**"I finished my chores…sir."
She finally spoke, her voice husky.
She cleared her throat. "What…
what else do you want from me?"
she finished, a hint of defiance
lighting her almond-shaped eyes.**

With her question, both his body and mind went into full-on battle. His mind told him that what he felt whenever he was around her didn't make any sense. Or the fact that she was on his mind twenty-four seven was something he needed to walk away from while he still could.

But his body told him it was time to show her, in detail, exactly what he wanted from her.

His gaze stole over her cheeks, which were stained with a hint of a flush; to her eyes, which were focused on his mouth.

His body

He placed and tunneled th drils of hair at the b tugged her body until she was pressed against his.

Before she could catalog in her mind the clarity of his intent, he'd brought his mouth down and covered hers.

Books by Kimberly Kaye Terry

Kimani Romance

Hot to Touch
To Tempt a Wilde

KIMBERLY KAYE TERRY's

love for reading romances began at an early age. Long into the night she would stay up until she reached "The End" with her Mickey Mouse night-light on, praying she wouldn't be caught reading what her mother called "those" types of books. Often, she would acquire her stash of "those" books from beneath her mother's bed. Ahem. To date, she's an award-winning author of fourteen novels in romance and erotic romance, has garnered acclaim for her work and happily calls writing her full-time job.

Kimberly has a bachelor's in social work and a master's in human relations and has held licenses in social work and mental-health therapy throughout the United States and abroad. She volunteers weekly at various social service agencies and is a long-standing member of Zeta Phi Beta Sorority, Inc, a community-conscious organization. Kimberly is a naturalist and practices aromatherapy. She believes in embracing the powerful woman within each of us and meditates on a regular basis. Kimberly would love to hear from you. Visit her at www.kimberlykayeterry.com.

To Tempt a
WILDE

Kimberly Kaye Terry

KIMANI™
ROMANCE

To my amazing daughter,
who inspires me to be the best that I can be.

KIMANI PRESS™

Recycling programs
for this product may
not exist in your area.

ISBN-13: 978-0-373-86201-6

TO TEMPT A WILDE

Dear Reader,

I'm very pleased to introduce to you Nate Wilde and Althea Hudson, the hero and heroine from *To Tempt a Wilde,* the first couple in my new family miniseries, Wyoming Wilde. Writing their story was an exciting learning experience for me, as I had the opportunity to see through the eyes of my heroine what it was like to find, rope and rein in her very own cowboy!

Learning of her father's death, Althea has been on the run for two years from the man responsible for it, afraid for her life. Her running sends her straight into the arms of sexy cowboy Nate Wilde, the eldest of three brothers who own and run one of the largest cattle ranches in the West.

Nate is determined to keep his mind—and his heart—firmly guarded against the woman with a hidden past. But this becomes harder and harder with each scalding-hot encounter. It's not long before they both succumb to a love worth fighting for.

As always, I appreciate your support and will do my best to continue writing deliciously hot and sexy stories featuring alpha men and the women they love! Look for Holt and Yasmine's story in *To Desire a Wilde,* coming April 2011!

Keep it sexy! ;)

Kimberly

Chapter 1

The sliver of light peeking between the cracked window blinds drew him like a magnet.

He'd had no intention of doing anything besides sitting in the car this time. Knowing that she was nearby and that if he'd *wanted* to go to her he could had been good enough.

But the minute he saw the light flicker on inside her room, he had been helpless to resist. It was as though she knew he was there.

That she was inviting him to come closer.

He cut the engine on the car.

Pulling his leather coat over his slim body, he then tugged on the matching kid-leather gloves and grabbed the dark knit hat on the passenger side and pulled it over his head, both for protection against the frigid cold and as a means of disguise.

But he doubted anyone could identify him. Or even

knew who he was for that matter. But he was always careful.

Always.

Lifting the binoculars from around his neck, he pocketed them and left the car. Inching his way toward her window, he stealthily made for the light beckoning him.

As he moved closer, he cast furtive glances over his shoulder just to make *sure* no one was watching.

As if anyone cared what the hell happened in this godforsaken place, he thought in disgust, wrinkling his nose, the ends of his fine nostrils flaring.

He stopped when he reached a large Dumpster several feet away from her window and withdrew the binoculars from his pocket.

He wouldn't get too close. Not yet. He didn't want to chance her seeing him, not before he was ready. Once he had her, she would be his. This time forever.

His full lips split into a wide grin in anticipation of the time to come when he and his baby would be reunited.

The excitement he felt at the thought of their reunion made him so excited he had to take deep, calming, measured breaths. His hand snaked down to the front of his slacks, unconsciously running it over the slight bulge pressing insistently against his zipper.

The sound of a child wailing startled him, making him drop the binoculars he held, his hand quickly moving away from his groin. With a curse he quickly retrieved the binoculars, grinding his teeth in anger.

It had been a long time since he'd been this close to

her. In his excitement he could get careless. He needed to get it together.

He waited a bit longer before bringing the binoculars to his eyes. He barely held back a groan of delight when the new angle gave him an even *better* view of her.

Oh, God, she was beautiful. Even in silhouette she was beautiful.

He crouched down when he heard footsteps behind him. A swift glance over his shoulder revealed a young man and woman strolling his way. He slid behind the funky trash bin, again not taking the chance that anyone would see him.

He bit back a curse when the two lovers stopped less than a foot away from him and decided *that* was the spot to play grab-ass.

He held his breath as long as he could, trying not to gag on the offensive smell from the Dumpster, until the couple finally broke from their embrace and ambled away.

Bringing the binoculars to his eyes again, he brought her room back into view, cursing when she was no longer standing in front of the window. The room was once again bathed in darkness.

Not only had she turned off the light, but she'd also drawn the curtains. Damn it.

He waited a few minutes more in the hopes she'd get up again when he heard more footsteps coming his way.

What the hell…didn't these people have to get up in the morning? Didn't they have jobs to go to? His mental tirade came to a halt as he glanced around.

With a sneer he remembered *what* type of neighborhood he was in. Ninety percent of the residents were on welfare and the other ten percent held a job just long enough to draw unemployment.

The sneer turned to righteous anger when he thought of Althea choosing to live among people like *these,* instead of with him.

But all of that would change soon.

Soon he'd have his baby back where she belonged, by his side, living the way she was used to. Soon everything would be back to normal.

And he'd make sure she would never leave him again.

Althea sat straight up in bed, her heart thumping hard against her chest.

She cast a glance around the tiny hotel room and moistened her dry lips with her tongue.

The shadows in the room seemed to be mocking her, laughing at her. Her hand lingered over her heart as though that would calm its frantic hammering.

Turning to the small lamp set atop the scarred table, she flipped it on. It flickered a few times before dying.

"Damn, not again," she muttered, before grabbing the baseball bat that lay beside her, throwing her legs over the side of the bed and rising.

She breathed a short sigh of relief when she turned on the wall switch and the room was instantly washed in light.

Pulling her sweat jacket from the foot of the bed she drew it over her body and pulled up the zipper, then stuffed her feet inside her sneakers.

She checked the tiny living/bedroom area first before walking to the kitchen. Although she felt foolish, she opened each of the cabinets and peered inside. She'd once made the mistake of not checking a small area.

She fingered the scar near her temple, just above her hairline. She'd never make that mistake again.

Briskly she walked the short distance to the bathroom and turned on the light, cautiously walking into the bathroom. With the bat clenched tightly in her hands, she pushed the paper-thin, cracked shower curtain out of the way and peered inside.

All clear. She blew out a breath of relief she didn't know she'd been holding.

Slowly she made her way back to the main living area, her routine completed. The routine was as familiar as it was depressing. She relaxed the death grip she held on the bat, glancing around the room once more. There was nothing else to check.

Everything was the same way it had looked when she'd finally gone to sleep. When she'd checked in a few weeks back, the motel had boasted of a spacious living room and dining area, as well as a kitchenette.

She eyed the room, one brow arching.

The "spacious" living room was actually one room, featuring a bed, a ratty, stained corner chair and round table next to it, which separated the dual room from the even smaller kitchenette. The kitchenette consisted of two overhead cabinets stationed above a minuscule oven, on which only one of the burners worked. The refrigerator was a small cube with barely enough room to store the bare essentials.

She'd had more room in her bedroom closet at one time than in her entire current living space.

She glanced over at the radio clock near the narrow bed…it was two-thirty-two in the morning. This time she'd managed to get a whole four hours of straight sleep.

That hadn't happened in over a month.

She hesitated, looking over at the small window in the room. With a sigh she walked over and slipped her fingers through the cracked venetian blinds before peering through them, her gaze sweeping over the outside view.

What a view, she thought, shaking her head. A Dumpster was less than five feet away, the smell it emitted was one she tried to combat with scented plug-ins and incense. None of which had made a bit of difference as the faint scent of eau de funk flavored the room no matter what she did. She glanced over at the parking lot, with its odd assortment of beat-up cars and those that looked so out of place it hadn't taken too much of a guess to figure out what the owners did to afford such vehicles in the poor neighborhood.

Despite the feeling that someone was out there, watching her, the only thing Althea saw was a young couple strolling along the sidewalk. She reclosed the blinds, walked over to the bed and sat down, holding the bat loosely in her hands, tapping the end against her palm.

She leaned over, opened the drawer and withdrew her wallet, pulling out the money inside. She began recounting it, although she already knew how much she had, down to the penny: five hundred twenty-one dollars and thirteen cents.

There was a time when she had never given a thought to how much money she had on hand, hadn't worried where she would lay her head next, or where she'd live.

Those times seemed as though they'd happened in another lifetime, to another woman.

She glanced down at her hands as she held the money, felt the calluses that were now permanent fixtures on them, before placing the money back inside the drawer. At least she had some money on hand, for when the time came to move on.

She liked the sleepy, small town of Billings, Montana. She'd been there for three weeks, and had been waitressing at a local café/truck stop for two of those weeks, twelve-hour shifts straight, in order to save as much money as she could in as short a time as possible.

Althea never knew when she'd have to go back on the run. One week, two weeks or a month.

She'd learned to do whatever it took, take whatever job, no matter how menial, in order to survive.

Although the hours were usually long, and her muscles ached so badly all she could do when she got off work was lie down with a heating pad on her back to ease the pain, she enjoyed the odd jobs. Enjoyed the freedom, the anonymity.

Althea laughed softly, thinking how she would never have imagined she would actually *enjoy* doing physical labor. Doing work she would have previously thought beneath her. Or that she would enjoy being alone and not on the social scene.

Life changes. Dreams change.

Dream as if you'll live forever, live as if you'll die today.

The ghost of a smile died from her lips as one of her father's favorite sayings came to her mind.

With a sigh, Althea lay back against the thin headboard. So much for her long-ago dreams.

She was tired of running. But she never ignored her instincts. And her instincts were telling her it was time to go.

But where do I go now?

She unzipped her jacket, and as she tossed it to the foot of the bed, a business card fell from the pocket. As Althea reached over and picked up the card, her brows knitted. Beneath an engraved crest were two Ws linked and the name Wyoming Wilde Ranch in bold script centered on the card.

Thinking of the two brothers who had come into the café a few days ago, she frowned. The two men hadn't looked like brothers to her; one was white and the other Native American. Yet when they'd told her who they were and that they owned a ranch outside of Landers, Wyoming, she'd not asked any questions. That too was something she'd learned not to do. Ask as few questions as possible and stick to herself...keep her head low.

The men had been to the café twice in the last week. If it had been a different time in her life...well, she would have had a different reaction to the casual offer both of the good-looking brothers had made to take her out. Although different as day and night, the one thing the brothers had in common had been that they both seemed to take up *all* the testosterone in the room. A ghost of a smile lifted the corner of her mouth in appreciation.

She'd been reading the local paper when they'd come inside the café the last time, checking out the want ads when one of them—she scrunched her brows—Shilah, the Native American brother, asked her if she was looking for work.

She'd smiled and made an offhand comment that she was always looking for work. An odd expression had crossed his handsome face before he'd told her they were in need of help around the ranch.

He'd told her the ranch was located in Wyoming and the work was only seasonal, but if she were interested…

Although always on the lookout for opportunities, in case she had to leave suddenly, Althea had shied away from answering him. The intensity in his eyes was unnerving; it was as though he were seeing straight to the heart of her, as though he'd read things she didn't want anyone to know.

She'd thanked him but told him she wasn't ready to relocate.

He'd opened his mouth as though to speak when she caught the subtle nudge from his brother and a shake of his head. Instead of speaking, he'd handed her his card, telling her the offer would be open if she ever wanted it.

She'd glanced up an hour later and had noted the men leaving, a part of her regretting her decision not to hear more about the job.

Glancing down at the card now, Althea ran her fingers over the raised crest, the looped Ws that resembled a rope, lost in thought.

Welcome to the Wilde side of ranching.

She rose from the bed and turned off the light. Before she did, she glanced back toward the window, a shiver running through her.

Again she raised a hand and ran trembling fingers over the small scar that spanned no more than an inch near her hairline. She'd learned one thing over the last two years: trust her instincts.

Her instincts were telling her—no, *screaming* at her—that it was time to go. And go now.

Chapter 2

Nathan Wilde wanted nothing more than to put his feet up, pop open a can of beer and relax, exhausted and sweaty from moving cattle to the spring pasture for the better part of the day with his brothers.

"No beer for you, but I'm sure oats and water will work just the same, right, girl?" he asked, affectionately patting the rear end of the horse he'd just dismounted.

After walking, watering and patting down Gerry, his favorite workhorse, Nate strapped the canvas feeding bag over her neck and led her to the stables.

Running a weary hand over the back of his neck, he rolled his shoulders forward, trying to work out the knots settled deep. As soon as their workday ended, his brothers had decided to go into town to their favorite sports bar to unwind, inviting Nate to go with them.

According to them, a woman was all a man needed to work out his "knots." Although they'd issued the invitation, they'd done so more out of habit rather than any real belief that Nate would actually accept. They, like Nate, knew what his automatic response would be; not only no, but hell, no.

A woman was the last thing he wanted to work out his knots. He could do without the hassle of what came *after* a woman worked out his knots.

Nate led the horse toward the stable, thinking of his brothers' invitation. There was a time when all three of them had been called the Wilde boys for a reason, besides it being their last name. They worked hard and played just as hard, and any woman knew when dealing with the men that that was all it was—play. It had been that way for Nate until two years ago…

He shook his head. A lot had changed since then.

When he'd gone too long without a woman and his need was rising high—that was the only time he ventured into town and went on the hunt. Those times he made sure the woman he chose knew the score from jump.

He was looking for a one-time thing. Just a hard, hot ride to release his pent-up energy. And nothing more. No expectations or demands on either side.

As he was pushing open the double-sided stable door to lead Gerry inside, he paused with one foot inside the barn. The low hum of a woman's voice stopped him dead in his tracks and pulled him out of his mental musings.

With a frown on his face, Nate cautiously moved forward, Gerry docilely trailing behind him.

"Yes, baby, you are a beauty aren't you?" the unknown woman crooned, her voice low, soothing.

Frown still in place, Nate led the horse to her stall and opened the gate, ushering her inside. He gave her one more absentminded pat on the rear before locking the gate and moving toward the voice.

The woman's soft voice echoed in the quiet stable, tugging at Nate, and his feet moved as though of their own volition, drawing him closer to the source. When he came to the open stalled area he stopped, his eyes narrowing.

Standing before the Arabian palomino he'd recently purchased was a woman, the top of her head barely reaching the horse at mane level.

Her face was turned slightly away from him as she ran a small hand over the horse's neck, down her side. As she whispered soothing words, the horse's willingness to allow her to touch him fascinated Nate.

He'd recently purchased the horse from a rancher who'd put up his livestock for sale after selling his spread to a major conglomeration for a hefty fee. Although he'd owned mostly cattle, he'd also sold several horses. However, the palomino remained.

The old rancher had rescued it from a shelter that recovered abused horses and sought to rehabilitate them. Eventually the man had given up trying to tame the beast, unable to get anywhere near the animal besides to feed him.

Nate had gone to the ranch for the sole purpose of purchasing the Braunvieh bulls, paying a hefty price for several of the bulls to breed with their Angus. Yet when the rancher had shown him the stables and the last remaining horse for sale, he'd bought the horse, too.

It was beautiful and wild.

Beyond the fear, there was a keen intelligence in the horse's watchful gaze, and Nate knew he had to buy it, convinced he could get to the animal, earn its trust. Nate had been sure that with the right touch, the beautiful horse would eventually come around.

In the week since the horse had been delivered, Nate hadn't been able to get within two feet of the damn thing without it neighing, kicking its feet up and pitching a damn fit.

Last time he'd tried, he'd come in serious danger of losing his ability to father children….

And now, to witness this small, unknown woman uttering soothing nonsense at the horse, and it not only allowing, but encouraging her, nuzzling against her hand, was nothing short of amazing to Nate.

He leaned against the wall, crossing his arms over his broad chest, and watched the interaction between the semiwild horse and the woman, listening as she spoke, a deep frown pulling his brows together.

Althea hadn't been so…at ease, in a long time.

She inhaled a deep breath, a smile tilting one corner of her mouth up slightly. Even the air smelled better. Cleaner, new. Alive.

That was it. That's what was different.

She hadn't felt so alive as she did here at Wyoming Wilde. Hadn't felt so protected as she did now in longer than she wanted to remember.

Although the ranch was accessible, no one set foot on the property who wasn't invited. And no one came without at least ten men knowing of their arrival.

Continuing to smooth her hands over the beautiful

horse's mane, she thought of her short time at Wyoming Wilde Ranch.

The morning she'd awakened from the night when she'd felt someone watching her, she'd known it was time for her to move on.

Not that she'd gotten any sleep after she'd turned off the light.

Instead she'd alternated between staring up at the ceiling, watching the blades on the old ceiling fan swirl round and round, the loud hum fading into the background, and fingering the business card she held clutched in her hand.

Finally she'd given up on sleep, just as the early-morning sunrise was peeking through the cracked blinds. She'd risen and brewed a cup of coffee before sitting down at the beat-up kitchen table. Thoughtfully, she'd sipped the strong brew while contemplating what her next move would be.

Glancing down at the card she'd laid on the table, Althea had made up her mind. Wyoming Wilde…she was going to the ranch. Why not? She'd gone on flimsier leads than that in her two years of moving from place to place.

She'd packed her scanty belongings before going by the diner to inform her boss that she was quitting.

That had been the hardest part of her decision.

The harried cook/owner had begged Althea to stay longer, at least for a few more nights, so he could find another waitress to help them out. Business was booming, as many ranchers and farmers from the surrounding areas were moving cattle and purchasing new stock, which meant traveling and stopping by the café.

Althea had been close to agreeing, mainly because the owner had been good to her, paying her weekly wages in cash versus a check without deeply questioning her reasons. That and the desire to get another few more days of tips had made her debate her decision to leave that day.

Piggybacking that thought, Althea had again gotten that eerie feeling of being watched.

She'd glanced nervously around the busy café, surveying the late-morning crowd. She'd seen no signs of anyone paying her any particular attention, yet remembering the previous night's unease had been enough to strengthen her resolve to go.

When he'd realized Althea wasn't going to waver, he'd asked her where she was headed, a concerned look crossing his deeply lined face. Althea had plastered a wide smile on her face, hoping the strain of what she really felt wasn't showing, and told him she was headed east, that a friend had opened up a new restaurant and she had agreed to help.

The lie tripped smoothly from her lips, and she squelched down the guilt she felt. Mason was one of the few people she'd worked for who she'd actually begun to get close to.

Although she hadn't dared share her history with him, or even tell him her full name, after the diner closed she and the older man had fallen into an easy, unexpected camaraderie.

He'd given her a look, one that had spoken volumes, and she'd squirmed a bit beneath his scrutinizing stare, but he hadn't asked any more questions and had walked to the back to retrieve her pay, handing it to her and giving her an awkward hug goodbye.

It wasn't until she was in her car that she opened the envelope, a small smile of gratitude crossing her full lips. Besides her wages, Mason had added several more crisp one-hundred-dollar bills, along with a note telling her to be safe.

Althea stifled the tears that threatened to fall.

She'd then gassed up at the Gas 'n Go next to the diner, bought a few necessities and hopped inside her car, preparing to leave.

That eerie feeling had crept over her again. She'd glanced into her rearview mirror, a shiver running over her spine, her heartbeat speeding up and thumping hard against her chest when she caught site of a dark green Mercedes coupe pulling into the diner as she left the gas station. The same make and color as the car *he* drove.

Keeping the car in sight as it came to a smooth halt, she'd watched a woman come from within, her high heels sinking into the unpaved parking lot as she walked inside the diner. Even though it wasn't him, Althea's instincts told her that he wasn't far away.

He never was.

Without hesitating, she'd peeled out of the gravel parking lot and quickly headed east on I-90, once again on the move.

Now, as Althea heard the deep voice speak behind her, she spun around, her heart racing. She automatically stepped back several steps, warily glancing around looking for the can of mace she always carried and had placed near her feet when she'd entered the horse's stall.

She eased her body down as subtly as possible and grabbed the can, palming it within her hand.

The man's head swiveled, looked down at her hand before looking back at her. Although his eyes were shadowed beneath the Stetson he wore low on his head, leaving only a pair of well-defined, sensual lips visible, she *felt* his stare. She swallowed nervously.

She stood and glanced up, way up, as he pushed away from the wall and ambled toward her.

"What the hell are you doing with my horse…and who the hell let you in here?"

The question was spoken in a low, deep rumble. Yet the smooth tone did *nothing* to disguise the distinct… *menacing* undertone.

Althea's heart leaped wildly against her chest as she stepped back, stopping only when her back brushed against the end of the stall.

Caught, unable to move away any farther, her tongue came out to moisten her bottom lip.

Waiting for the fear to come, Althea wondered why instead she felt a feminine rush of awareness sliver along her spine as he advanced into the stall.

Chapter 3

Nate advanced farther into the stall.

His glance raked over the woman in one all-encompassing glance, from her long dark brown hair, pulled up into a messy ponytail, down over a snug-fitting T-shirt that molded her small, high breasts.

His gaze then rolled over her long, jeans-clad legs and back up again, sliding over her face, cataloging each of her features slowly.

To say she was beautiful was too...weak a description.

Her features were perfectly spaced in her oval face; eyes so dark they appeared black, wide-set and faintly tilted in the corners. Her nose was narrow, with a slight flare at the ends of her nostrils.

But it was her mouth that caught his attention, pulled him up short and made his cock thump against his zipper.

Both lips were full, wide and sensual. And made his

mind wander, for a split second, thinking of how they'd feel against his mouth, on his body…

Her skin was the color of rich, dark honey, smooth and flawless. Decadent.

His hands itched to run down the side of her face, down her throat. His tongue tingled, irrationally, with a need to trace it down the smooth column of her neck. To find out if it tasted as good as it looked.

The thoughts came out of nowhere, bringing him up short.

Damn. Maybe his brothers were right. Maybe it *had* been too long since he'd been with a woman.

His eyes met hers.

Something tangible yet elusive passed between them as they made their silent observations of each other. Although her expression remained neutral, he caught the flicker of awareness in the dark depths of her eyes.

The horse whinnied in the background, breaking the intense, sudden connection, dragging Nate's attention away from the woman in front of him.

A glance toward the horse showed it pawing at the ground before tossing its head back in a jerky movement. The ends of its nostrils flared as it kept its gaze on Nate. The animal had picked up on the sudden tension in the stable. Nate took a cautious step toward the near-wild beast.

When he brought his hand up to reassure the animal its neighing became louder as it pawed the ground, growing more agitated.

The woman turned toward the horse and laid a hand over its hind end, her lips pursing, making a calming, shushing sound. Immediately the horse quieted, but still it kept its amber-colored eyes on Nate, backing away from him until it stood between the two of them. The animal didn't stop until it had positioned itself directly in front of her, as though it was protecting her from him.

He saw the ghost of a smile break across the woman's full mouth, tilting one side up, a glint of what looked like humor sparking in her dark eyes, surprising him. Again, he felt his body's response, but ignored it.

He brought his hand to the brim of his Stetson, tilting it in her direction.

"My name is Nathan. Nathan Wilde. What the hell are you doing in my stables, with my horse?" he asked.

When the tall cowboy tilted his hat toward her, the gesture oddly old-fashioned yet appealing to Althea, she slowly eased away from the wall, her hand remaining on the horse, soothing it.

"My name is Althea. Althea…Dayton."

She hoped he didn't catch the hesitation. She'd used her mother's maiden name, which was her middle name, for the last two years, as a means of helping to keep under the radar. The fact that she hesitated even that small bit was unnerving to her, something she'd never done before. The fact that he could rattle her enough to cause the small slip-up was even more disturbing to Althea.

When he removed his hat his face was fully revealed. Althea drew in a swift breath, slowly expelling it.

To say he was handsome was too mild…too *tame* a description for the man standing in front of her.

He exuded raw, male earthiness in scalding waves. His skin, the color of molten chocolate, made her want to reach out and run her fingers over his face…she barely resisted the urge. She continued to keep her hand on the horse, thankful for its presence.

So this was Nathan Wilde, the oldest of the Wilde brothers, the one she'd heard about but had yet to meet.

When she'd arrived a few days before she'd been introduced to the men who worked the ranch, hiding her surprise when there'd only been one female who worked for Wilde Ranch, the housekeeper, Lilly. Lilly had been the one to take her to the guest cottage she'd live in during her stay. The older black woman had been open and friendly as she showed Althea around, her love for the ranch obvious in the pride in her expression.

After that, she'd been given the full tour of the ranch by Holt and Shilah, which had taken the majority of the day, as their land and livestock spread over two hundred acres.

The brothers had mentioned their oldest brother, Nathan, only briefly, simply telling her he was away buying cattle and wouldn't return until the end of the week.

"Too late for him to do anything about it then," Holt had said, turning to his brother. Althea's radar had gone on full alert at the comment, knowing it had something to do with her, but she hadn't asked. She'd simply filed it in the back of her mind for later thought.

They'd given her three weeks pay upfront, no strings attached, something that surprised Althea but at the same time made her instantly at ease, just in case she had to move on unexpectedly.

Later that evening, after the men had shown her

around, she'd gone to the main house where Lilly had invited her to eat. Not having had the opportunity to go into Landers and pick up supplies, she'd been thankful for the invitation.

Remembering Holt's earlier comment, she'd casually mentioned it to the older woman, watching her as she bustled around the kitchen, removing a storage bowl from the refrigerator to heat up leftover food from the afternoon meal for Althea.

The older woman had paused, one hand on the chrome handle of the microwave, and glanced at Althea. She'd held her gaze for such a long time that Althea had immediately regretted her impulse in bringing up the question.

"Baby, did you notice there weren't any women working on the ranch?" She finally spoke, closing the door and setting the cook time.

Althea nodded her head, slowly.

"There's a good reason for that," she'd said, her expression, although light, serious as she turned and fully faced Althea.

"And that would be?"

The older woman turned away, moving toward the stove to pour the boiling water into two mugs she'd set out before tossing tea bags into both.

"Besides me, you're the first woman in over two years who's been on the ranch. Let's just say women living at the Wilde Ranch has never been an…easy thing."

Before Althea could digest that comment, the older woman had continued. "And if you want to stay for any amount of time, my suggestion would be to lay low, do your job and everything will be fine. Particularly around Nate."

Something in the woman's expression warned her not to ask questions, so she simply nodded her head and sipped the tea Lilly placed in front of her, feeling a kernel of apprehension knot in her belly for the first time in the week she'd been on the ranch.

Now she straightened, dusted her hand down the side of her jeans and cautiously extended it toward him.

He glanced down at her hand and hesitated for a fraction of a second before he engulfed it within his large one. Althea did everything she could not to squirm, the electric heat of his hand touching hers, warming her on contact, sparking off a fizzle of awareness down her spine.

"Yes, Mr. Wilde, I've heard about you, from your brothers. What I meant was, your brothers told me you were away when they hired me. Not that that was the reason they hired me or anything. I just…" She stopped, took a breath, trying like hell to curb her nervous chatter. "I look forward to working here at the ranch." She rushed out the rest of the sentence, expelling the breath of air she'd taken as she did.

He held her hand, held it a fraction longer than was necessary before slowly releasing it.

"It's beautiful here, I've already started falling in love with—"

"No offense, Ms.…Dayton," he broke in, eyes narrowing, cutting Althea off, making her want to bite her tongue for the words she blurted and her crazy inability to stop with the nervous chatter.

She didn't miss the emphasis he'd placed on her last name. As though he suspected she hadn't given him her true name.

But his voice, smooth and liquid, distracted her momentarily. He had the type of voice that inexplicably brought out *everything* feminine in her. Things she thought long buried deep down inside, things she thought she'd never feel, tucked deep.

Her imagination took over as she eyed him. She imaged him roping cattle on a lazy summer day, beads of sweat glistening against his naked, muscled chest, wearing snug low-riding jeans, his Stetson on, the rim low, shading his eyes…

"But as my brothers should have consulted with me before hiring you, I'm not so sure your stay here will *be* that long. I wouldn't want you to fall too deeply in love. With the ranch, that is," he said, breaking into her little fantasy and bringing a flush to her face, dragging her mind away from the unexpected flight it had taken.

Althea withdrew her hand from his and fully faced him, swallowing down her embarrassment.

The noticeable coolness in his tone was in direct competition with the heated way he was looking at her, the way he'd been since the moment he entered the stall. His words said one thing, his eyes something totally different.

Althea focused on what had just flown out of his mouth.

"Well, Mr. Wilde, as your brothers were so kind as to give me three weeks' pay—" she began, and ignored the look of surprise on his face "—for the next three weeks at least, you don't have one damn thing to say about that," she finished, and smoothly turned away from him, giving the horse her full attention.

Before she turned away she saw the flash of irritation on his face and squelched the need to laugh. She had enough sense to know when to walk away from a fight. No sense in pulling the lion's tail any more than she had today.

"We'll see about that," he nearly growled, advancing on her.

Hot and heavy, the tension instantly grew thick; heady and palpable.

Althea, despite the way the last years had shaken out, forcing her into hiding, had never been one to run from a challenge.

"Either I can work off the advance, or I can leave. Either way I'm fine with it. I'm *still* getting paid. It's your call."

So much for not pulling the lion's tail, she thought with a mental shrug.

With her heartbeat racing out of control, Althea felt his glare on her the entire time as she turned and gave the horse a final pat, pretending a nonchalance she didn't feel.

As quickly as humanly possible she was out of the stable, not waiting around to see his reaction to her challenge…wondering what in the name of God she'd just signed on for.

Chapter 4

"Either I can work off the advance or leave. Either way I'm fine with it..."

A deep frown settled between Nate's brows as he drove past the south pasture heading into town, thinking of the words slung at him by the woman.

He hadn't wanted to go to town. He had enough to do around the ranch to keep him busy from sunup to sundown. But thoughts of the woman—Althea—had plagued him the entire morning.

Hell, thoughts of her and their exchange had kept him up most of the night as well.

Although she'd said it in an "I don't give a damn" kind of way, he'd seen a look akin to desperation in her eyes. The look, coupled with his reaction to her, had plagued him throughout the night and into the next day.

One time too many while helping the hands mend

some critical fence, he'd had to redo a piece he'd fixed. Once he'd nearly hammered off his own finger as he pounded away at the fencing before he decided he needed to get away.

Immediately images assaulted his mind in vivid, erotic detail of just *how* Ms. Althea Dayton, or whatever her real name was, could work out the debt.

Vivid, mind-blowing images.

The type that even now had his cock rock-hard and ready. Ready to show the smug woman just *how* she could service him.

His mood had gone from hell to hell-in-a-handbasket when he'd stalked inside the house and caught his brothers before they could make a quick getaway.

Nate stopped just inside the doorway and surveyed the scene in front of him. Both of his brothers were eating the jumbo cookies Lilly had made. Praising her for them as though they'd never tasted a damn cookie before. Relaxed as though they hadn't a care in the world.

To say he was pissed off was putting it mildly.

"Okay, who the hell's bright idea was it to hire that *woman* and not let me know about it?"

The conversation came to a grinding halt in the warm, airy kitchen as soon as he spoke.

His brothers looked up at him, cookies halfway to their mouths, both looking as guilty as two boys with their hands caught in the cookie jar.

One look at Nate's angry, tight features and they knew, instantly, they were in deep-shit trouble.

A side glance in Lilly's direction and Nate had seen the humor lurking in her dark eyes but had chosen to ignore it. Miss Lilly could find humor in the situation. She had that right. He couldn't go off half-cocked with the woman who'd helped raise him, one who was like a surrogate mother.

He turned back to his brothers.

They, on the other hand, didn't get a get-out-of-jail-free card. Not even close.

"Don't even *try* getting away," he said, pinning them with a look when they both, at the same time, made as though to leave the room.

Both Shilah and Holt paused midflight. Slowly, they spun around on the scuffed-up heels of their well-worn boots, both warily watching him as he advanced farther into the large kitchen.

He stopped less than a foot from them, crossed his arms over his wide chest and stared them down.

Although technically there wasn't much in the way of staring down. The men were all of similar height, Holt being the tallest at six foot five, Nate and Shilah just a few inches shy of that.

"Okay, now look here, brother—" Holt was the first to speak in his slow, crawling drawl, the one he used when he was either trying to get a piece of tail from a woman or when he knew he'd screwed up and was buying time.

"Cut the brother crap," Nate interrupted. That was another thing he did. Whenever he wanted to maneuver his way out of a situation, Holt was quick to pull out the brother card.

"Besides, it wasn't me who invited her to come. It was Shilah—"

"Way to throw me under the bus," Shilah broke in, his

expression neutral, yet the look he gave Holt promised retribution was coming his way. Soon.

"I may have issued the initial invitation, but you were the one who actually hired her when she came."

"Yeah, well—"

Nate held up a hand, forestalling any more arguing on exactly *whose* fault it was.

"Whichever one of you—or both of you—is to blame, I don't give a damn. Just take care of the problem. Now."

"And how do you want us to do that? We've already paid her in advance."

"So I heard," Nate replied tightly.

"Besides, we need the help, you know that, Holt," Shilah said, always the one to use logic in any situation. "Lilly's surgery is in a few weeks and we can't spare any of the hands to help out. It's just temporary. She can do the odd jobs. Can help Lilly out in the kitchen—"

"Hell, no, she's not working in the kitchen. That's out," Nate bit out, the thought of the woman actually in his home, in his domain, something he wasn't about to allow. "No matter how you reason this out, you both know how I feel about women on the ranch. I should have been consulted."

There was a short pause, none of the men giving an inch, all staring each other down.

"How'd you find out, anyway?" Holt finally asked, running a hand over the back of his head.

"How long did you plan to hide it from me?" he asked, raising a brow. When Holt shrugged, his expression sheepish, Nate continued. "Walked into the stable where I've been keeping the new horse, and she was there, feeding it."

"Thought that horse didn't let anyone near her."

"She doesn't. Didn't," Nate corrected himself.

Thinking of how gentle the horse had been with the woman, the lines of his face wrinkled, momentarily making him forget his irritation with his brothers. "Damnedest thing, too. She was feeding it by hand. It was all but cuddling in her lap, like some kinda lap dog."

"Your problem is you don't know how to deal with a stubborn female. Horses are no different. You have to be gentle, say all the right things to her. Make her feel special."

"Oh, yeah, and I suppose you know how?"

"Damn right I do," Holt said, barking out a laugh. "You have to whisper in her ear, tell her how sweet her... tail is," he said, staring at his brother, laughter lurking in his eyes. "You do remember how to do that, right, Nate? Or do you need a crash course, brother? 'Cause if you do, I'm here for you, man...I'm here for you," he said, his voice lowering to a whisper, stringing out the last words.

"Yeah, I got your crash course right here," Nate replied, flipping his brother the bird. This time Holt openly laughed at him.

"You know what your problem is, Holt? You think everything is a damn joke," Nate bit out, and caught the gleam of humor in Shilah's eyes as well. This time he included him in his middle-finger salute as well.

"Since when do we need your permission to hire help around here?"

"Since the help you hired was a woman," he replied, not giving an inch. "I damn sure don't need another woman around here. Especially who, after realizing living on a ranch is not some bullshit Hollywood glamorized version, cuts out with the first man that comes her way."

"Man…what the hell?" Holt asked, frowning.

As soon as Nathan made the retort, he wanted to snatch the words back, feeling like a fool. He didn't need or want the pity he saw lurking in either one of his knuckle-headed brothers' eyes once it dawned on them what he'd said and why.

Holt grabbed the back of his neck again, rubbing it, his face reddening. "Yeah, well, sorry, bro. I guess I wasn't thinking. With Lilly about to have surgery in a few weeks and all, I figured she could use the help around the house. I wasn't trying to hurt you, you know that…" His voice trailed off into an awkward silence.

"You won't see much of her, anyway, Nate," Shilah said, pulling away from the wall he'd been leaning against. "You don't want her in the kitchen, that's cool. There's plenty of other things for her to do. And she's not staying in the main house. She's using the guest cottage. No worries. She'll only be here for a short time, just until Lilly has the surgery and is back on her feet. She'll be gone before you know it." Shilah finished.

Nate eyed him suspiciously, wondering at the swift change in attitude. Although he didn't like her using the guest cottage, the place he had built and planned to live in before Angela left, it was a better alternative to her living in his house. Under his roof.

Where he'd have easy access to her, night and day.

The errant thought blew across his mind before he could stop it, irritating him further.

"When you *boys* are done, dinner's in the oven. I'm going out to take the men their food, then I'm going to lie down before supper," Lilly interrupted before Nathan could speak.

All three men turned to look at her, completely forgetting her presence in the room as they argued, they were so used to her being around.

The emphasis she placed on calling them *boys* hadn't been lost on any of them.

"Let me help you with that, Ms. Lilly," Shilah said first, and she nodded her head toward the large covered dishes set on the counter. "Grab those."

"Truth be told, I *could* use a little help around here. That previous boy didn't last longer than a frog in heat; didn't know his butt from a hole in the ground *and* I ended up doing most of the work myself." She lifted the last dish from the oven and turned to place it on the stove. "I told you that boy was more trouble then he was worth. Don't know why you didn't hire that nice young woman from town like I told you to in the first place," she finished, staring a hole in Nate.

He felt all of ten years old, fighting the urge to duck his head in shame at the silent reprimand.

Lilly was going to have knee surgery in a few months, and with the date soon to arrive and lots of work to do, Nate had hired the young man to help with household chores, refusing to entertain the idea of hiring one of the local women from town at Lilly's suggestion.

He'd made no apologies for his "no woman hired" policy on the ranch, something everyone, including Lilly, had simply accepted as fact.

But now, with Lilly's silent reprimand, and the fact

that he'd probably made an ass of himself not only to the woman, but to his brothers about her being there, he knew he'd overreacted.

"You'd do well to give this one a chance, Nate. She actually looks like she understands the value of hard work. And sacrifice," she said, and after one more considering look added, "something you and your brothers know too well. Think about it before you throw her away." With that she turned and gathered the food, Shilah and Holt helping her, leaving Nate feeling like an idiot.

Now, as he drove into town, the entire situation was giving him a migraine he could damn well do without.

He floored the accelerator on his truck just as he was passing a cop, cursing when, after a glance in his rearview mirror, he caught sight of the cop peeling out from the side of the road and the accompanying flash of red lights.

Chapter 5

When Althea's radio alarm blared to life she woke up with a start, her heart thumping against her rib cage as the lyrics to the old Clash song "Should I Stay or Should I Go" blared loudly from the small speakers.

With a groan she slapped a hand over the knob, beating the alarm into silent submission.

"Should I stay or should I go?" She asked the question out loud, thinking how appropriate the lyrics to the song were in her current situation.

The light peeking through the wide slatted blinds cast a beautiful amber glow over the room.

Although she'd awakened to the sun rising often over the last two years, this one was different. It was as though it was embracing her, filling her with a "newness" that she hadn't felt in a long time.

She shook her head at her flight of fancy, but the smile on her face lingered as she stretched her back.

For once it didn't scream at her in pain. The muscles weren't tensed up as they usually were from a night spent on a bed that was either thin as paper or so lumpy it felt as though she'd slept on a bed of rocks all night.

Raising her arms above her head, she released a long, satisfying breath.

The bed she'd been sleeping on for the past week was queen-size with a thick, plush mattress, pulling a deep sigh of bliss from her lips.

She'd almost forgotten what it felt like to live decently.

No loud neighbors wakened her, either from cries of passion heard through the thin walls or screams and fighting, either. Nothing stopped her from getting a full eight hours of sleep. Not even her own mind.

After a week of this type of living, she knew she could get used to it.

The thought brought her eyes wide open and caused the smile to slip from her face. That kind of thinking was what she had to avoid.

Getting too comfortable in one place was something she couldn't afford to do. With a sigh, she placed her hands on the side of her and pushed herself into an upright position.

She'd used the alarm to wake her, realizing after the first three nights the ease with which she'd slept, surprised when her personal inner alarm allowed her to sleep past dawn, was both surprising and disturbing.

Her glance slid over the room.

She spied her baseball bat across the room, propped up against the wall. She'd even forgotten to place it near her as she'd gone to sleep last night.

She flipped her feet over the side of the bed and

rose. "Girl, you're getting soft," she murmured aloud to herself.

Althea headed toward the small, brightly lit kitchen to make tea, her bare feet sinking into the thick carpet, her mind on the changes in her life over the short time she'd lived at the ranch.

She'd been relieved when, after hiring her, the brothers had informed her she'd be staying in the guest cottage. It was close enough that the walk to the main house was only ten minutes but far enough way that she had a semblance of privacy.

It was an eclectic yet beautiful blending of rustic and contemporary design. Although no larger than fifteen hundred square feet, the open floor plan maximized the space, making full use of the living area and giving the cottage a larger feel.

The bedroom was sectioned off by five large floor-to-ceiling wood posts, and in the center of the room the queen sleigh-style bed was the focal point, its rich deep mahogany wood and scrolled etching unlike anything Althea had seen before.

In one corner was a stone-covered fireplace, similar to the one in the living area although slightly smaller, flanked by an antique-looking cheval mirror and Victorian-era chair that completed the furnishings.

There was a distinctly feminine touch to the room, making Althea wonder if a woman had had something to do with the decorating. Immediately she discounted the thought. With the way Nate Wilde had reacted to her, she doubted any woman, save Lilly, ever set foot in the cottage. At least not if he had anything to say about it.

The man obviously had issues.

As she walked through the cottage on her way to the kitchen, she glanced around the main living area. Although more rustic…masculine, in design, it too had a hint of softness, with its oversize furniture and ornately carved tables. As in the bedroom, there was a stone-covered fireplace, with a large, plush chocolate-brown rug set in front of it.

Althea paused, then walked over to the fireplace. Hunching down, she ran her hand over the soft pile, her fingers sinking deep into the fibers.

Out of nowhere came the image of her and Nathan Wilde sitting in front of the fireplace, drinking a glass of wine together, their bodies pressed close, their attention only on one another.

As soon as it did, she ridiculed herself for the fanciful image.

Nate Wilde had made it clear, in no uncertain terms, that he wanted nothing to do with her and if he had his way she'd be packed up and off the ranch, the sooner the better.

Not that she wanted him, even if he were so inclined.

She didn't know one thing about the man. Had only met him once.

What she did know was that he was arrogant and condescending. She also knew he had a chip on his shoulder about women that even a blind man could see.

And he was so different from the type of man she normally was attracted to it was ludicrous to even think of the two of them sharing a glass of wine, or anything else for that matter.

With an almost cruel clarity her body mocked her, her nipples tensing as thoughts of him barged their way into her mind. Forcing her to remember the way his aftershave, mixed with his body's natural scent, had blown across her senses, making her catch her breath when he'd stepped close to her inside the stall.

Or the look in his eyes when she'd issued the challenge to him. A look that said more than his words, one he probably wasn't aware of himself. One every woman knew the meaning of when it crossed a man's face.

She closed her eyes, took a deep breath.

Rising, she walked toward the kitchen, poured water in the kettle and set it on the stove while she stood staring out of the small window. She didn't know how long she stared outside, but the sound of the kettle whistling jarred her out of her thoughts. She poured the water into a mug, sunk a tea bag inside and sat down in one of the chairs at the dinette table.

Should she stay or should she go.

The lyrics of the song played around in her mind.

From the corner of her eye, she spied a penny lying on the carpet and rose slowly, walking over to it, a thoughtful frown on her face.

She lifted the coin from the carpet, fingering it.

"Heads I stay, tails I go. Seems a good enough way to decide as any," she said, laughing humorlessly.

Closing her eyes, she flipped the coin in the air, willing to allow fate to make the decision for her.

In what seemed to be slow motion she watched it spin in the air before it landed, soundlessly, on the thick carpet at her feet. She waited a full minute before glancing at it.

Heads.

She lifted the coin, palmed it in the center of her hand.

"Two out of three," she murmured.

Two more times the coin came up heads.

She sat back on her haunches, this time her laughter more relaxed. She shook her head. Not only because she was allowing a coin toss to decide her fate, but the fact that fate was *seriously* conspiring against her.

She took a deep breath, blew it out slowly and pulled herself together.

Despite everything that had happened to her over the past two years, she wasn't a quitter. She was tired of running. Damn tired. And this seemed to be the perfect place, if only for a short while, to take a break from running. Do some thinking about her life, figure out how to untangle the mess it had become.

And if Nate Wilde had a problem with that…well, she had tackled bigger obstacles in her life. He wasn't *anything* she couldn't handle.

After breakfast, Althea took a leisurely shower, smiling in bliss when she squirted the foamy, deeply scented bath gel onto her sponge, the rich, decadent lather smooth and silky against her skin.

Much like the rest of the cottage, the bathroom was fully stocked with everything from designer shampoos to the shower gel that felt like silk against her skin.

After indulging for longer than she should have in the shower, she quickly dried off, hurrying through the rest of her morning routine. When it came time to get dressed, she paused as she rifled through her meager possessions.

"Jeans, or jeans…or then again, there's jeans. Hmmm… what'll it be?" She tilted her head as though seriously considering her options. "Jeans it is," she said aloud, a reluctant laugh tumbling from her lips.

After lifting out the jeans, her hand brushed against her rare concession to feminine sensibility, one of only a few things she'd brought with her, nestled at the back of her drawer.

The proverbial little black dress.

She remembered the last time she'd worn it, at a black tie event with her father, the last one they'd been to together before he died. The smile drifted away from her face as she spied the small, framed photo of them she kept in the drawer. She lifted it and ran her thumb over his face.

"You look so handsome, Daddy," she whispered.

It was the last photo she had of herself and her father together. That night had been the last night she'd seen her father alive.

She closed her eyes briefly and placed the photograph back where she kept it.

Thinking of the man who'd stolen her life, her world made her clench her jaw tight and battle against tears that were never too far away, threatening to consume her if she allowed them to.

But she wouldn't. She couldn't.

Angrily Althea swiped the back of her hand across her eyes.

Tears weren't going to help her current situation, no more so than they could bring back her father. It was what it was, as that cliché saying went. But damn if it wasn't a hard, bitter pill to swallow.

She carefully refolded the dress and placed it at the back of the drawer, along with the photograph.

She quickly dressed, choosing her standard jeans, thermal undershirt and sweater, stuffed her feet inside her worn tennis shoes before grabbing her parka and heading out the door, putting her emotional armor in place, ready to face whatever the day…or Nate Wilde… dealt her.

Chapter 6

"Looks like Althea's working out pretty good. Don't you think?"

Nate threw his hat down on the sofa and strode toward the kitchen. Ignoring his brother, he opened the refrigerator and pulled out a Heineken. Turning, he offered the bottle up in the air, silently asking Holt if he wanted one.

"Thanks," he said, and caught the bottle as Nate tossed it his way, humor lurking in his blue eyes when he narrowly missed the bottle making a direct hit to his head.

Nate popped open the bottle top and raised it to his lips, ready to feel the cool amber liquid slide down his throat.

"Well?"

"Well, what?" he asked, eyeing his brother over the bottle.

"Can't you own up to the fact that you were wrong?"

Again, Nate ignored his brother. They'd agreed, by silent consent, to let the matter drop about Althea's working at the ranch. But that didn't mean he liked the idea now, any more than he had a week ago when he'd found her in his stable.

He'd just made damn sure she was nowhere near him at any given time.

"What's the real problem? And don't give me that bullshit that she's not pulling her weight…that horse won't fly."

Nate barely checked his anger. The less he showed Holt how much the woman in question was affecting him, the easier it would be to ignore the need to knock the Cheshire grin off his brother's face.

Only when he finished off the bottle did he answer, making sure he kept his face carefully neutral. "Wouldn't know. Haven't been paying attention."

The comment elicited a laugh from Holt. "Keep telling yourself that. Maybe you'll start to believe it," he said.

"From what the foreman says, she's been following him around. Hardly seems like she's earning the money you and Shilah decided to advance her."

"She's learning the job. Just like all the others who first come. And she's working hard, Nate. Damn hard," Holt said, his normal smirking humor missing, a seriousness taking its place.

Nate hid his surprise. Of the three of them, Holt was always the one with a ready joke, the one with the most laid-back sense of humor. If he didn't know better, he'd swear his brother was involved with the woman.

The thought brought on unreasonable and completely unexpected anger.

"Which one of you is interested in her?" He meant the question to come out lightly, but he heard the underlying anger himself and knew it hadn't escaped Holt's attention when he raised one blond brow.

"You need to give her a chance" was his only response.

That only added fuel to a fire already blazing out of control. He and Holt stared at one another, neither one giving an inch. "I don't need to give her anything. She's no different than any of the others. Make sure you remember that. Just give her the same jobs as any new recruit—"

"As in?" Holt broke in. "You won't let her near the house. Which makes no damn sense, as that's the reason we hired her, to help Lilly out. So what is it exactly that *you* want her to do?"

"Hell, I don't care, muck out the stalls for all I care, just give her a real job."

Holt lifted a brow. "Seriously? Man, are you serious? Muck the stalls? Who are you trying to turn her into, Nate, some kind of modern-day Cinderella?"

Holt kept his eyes on Nate, finished his beer and tossed the empty bottle in the recycle bin. Before he left he turned to face Nate again. "And I guess that would make you her knight in shining armor?" This time he laughed outright, his laughter booming off the walls when he gave Nate the "salute."

Once alone, with a disgusted snarl, Nate pushed away from the stool and stood.

"Okay Cinderella…time for you to do some real work; stay out of my way and out of my head."

* * *

Althea pushed the broom across the cement floor, pausing to wipe at the sweat that ran down her face, ran in rivulets down her neck and saturated the front of her T-shirt.

After reporting to the foreman yesterday, she'd been told there was to be a change in duties for her, which Althea was glad to learn. She didn't want anyone thinking she wasn't here to work. She'd been told that most of the men would be busy with other duties for the week, duties that didn't require her to watch and learn from them, and that she was going to be on her own.

She'd not even batted an eye when the older man, slightly red-faced, had told her what her job for the day was.

"Muck out the stalls? Seriously, I'm mucking out stalls," Althea mumbled aloud as she pushed the broom across the floor.

So it wasn't the most pleasant job she'd ever had, she thought, the musky smell making her wrinkle her nose. But she'd had worse jobs over the past two years. And she actually welcomed the hard work.

Yet she was under no illusions about whose idea this had been.

Her first day at the ranch, Shilah and Holt had allowed her to settle in, and the following days she'd alternated between helping Lilly in the kitchen and following one of the ranch hands, learning the operation. He'd not only showed her around but had also put her to work when she'd shown her competence at catching on quickly.

The work had been hard, and at the end of the day her muscles ached, but it had been a satisfying type of ache, the kind that came from doing something she'd found out she truly enjoyed doing, unlike the way she'd felt in her previous jobs.

Althea had felt a sense of pride at her accomplishments, although small, and found herself falling in love with the ranch with each passing day.

Now, as she pushed the wide brush broom over the cement floor, pausing to wipe away the sweat across her brow, a movement from her peripheral vision made her pause, her heartbeat strumming against her chest.

She placed the broom to the side and walked slowly toward the entry. She was out in one of the less populated areas of the ranch, alone with the exception of the few animals that grazed on the south pasture. Looking outside the opened double doors she scanned the area, seeing nothing more than what she'd expect, and slowly turned around and walked back inside, picking the broom back up and continuing.

She was alone. She shook off the nagging feeling, one she'd become used to, that hinted that he was just there, around the corner, ready to pounce.

He couldn't have found her. She'd been so careful this time. When she'd left Montana, she'd driven for miles in the opposite direction, checking her rearview mirror constantly to see if there was someone following her. Once she'd been assured there wasn't, she'd taken the turnaround and gone in the direction of the ranch.

Her hand brushed over the scar beneath the bangs she wore to hide it. She would never be caught unaware, ever again.

With a shaky sigh, Althea forced the painful memories away. As she worked, she still couldn't shake the feeling that she wasn't alone. On edge, she quickly went back to work cleaning and restocking the individual stalls with fresh hay.

A loud banging had her swinging around, broom in hand, clenched tightly and placed in front of her. Ready to fight, she spied a small cat scurrying away after toppling over one of the bales of hay.

"I've got to get it together. He's not here," she whispered, relaxing her grip on the broom.

Blowing out a sigh, she quickly finished. It was just nerves. She'd been on edge, the nagging feeling that she was being watched had started making her see things, thinking Reggie had somehow found her. And thoughts of Nate Wilde hadn't made it any easier.

She hadn't had an encounter with him in over a week, not since their first meeting. The few times she'd actually seen him, he'd seemed to go out of his way to avoid her. She would feel him watching her, a prickling awareness racing along her nerve endings would have her turning around to find the source. Not that she needed to. No one had ever had the type of effect on her that he had. It was as though some magnetic pull drew her to him, one she neither wanted nor needed in her life.

She'd had enough drama in her life to last a lifetime, she thought, finishing the last stall.

With the sun beginning to set, she wearily climbed onto the back of the horse she'd been assigned and made her way to the main house, pleased with the work she'd done but ready to go to the cottage, strip and take the longest, hottest shower of her life.

Dismounting, she led the horse to its stall, fed and

watered it and was walking toward her the cottage when Jake, the foreman, approached her.

"How'd it go today?"

"All done. Thought I'd make my way home…uh, to the cottage," she said, correcting herself before continuing, "and get something to eat."

"No problem. You can finish the rest tomorrow, it's no rush," he said, walking alongside her.

"Actually I'm done. Just finished the last one."

He stopped and frowned down at her. "You finished them all?" At her nod, his frown deepened. "Didn't expect you to do it all in one day, Ms. Althea. You had the week to finish," he said, and she laughed.

"Guess that means I'll get to laze around the pool the rest of the week then, huh?" she asked, a smile playing around her lips.

He grinned down at her. "Well…I can't offer you that, but why don't you come with me? A few of the men are trying to break in a new stallion. Stallion ain't having it. It always is a good time to see them try anyway," he said, laughing.

Although she wanted nothing more than to scrub the filth off her body, the thought of seeing something more exciting than horse poop all day had her agreeing, and she followed as he led her to a fenced-off area where several of the men were gathered.

Leaning against the wood fencing, Althea found herself laughing out loud along with the others as one by one the men lined up against the corral took their turn at trying to break in the wild stallion, none managing to stay on for more than a few seconds before being bucked off.

Mid-laugh her body suddenly tensed. That unwanted yet familiar feeling of being watched washed over her again, this time sending a fresh wave of chill bumps to dance along her body.

Althea turned, already knowing who was the one to cause her body to react on cue: Nate Wilde.

Standing less than one hundred feet away, he stood there. Just watching her.

His glance slid over her, starting at the top of her head, working its way down and over her body, the look so…electric Althea inhaled a swift breath.

She resisted the urge to touch her hair, tuck the strands she knew were sticking out everywhere back into the ponytail she'd put it into in the morning. Her mouth grew dry, and her tongue came out to moisten her lips.

His gaze followed the action, his look intense, even from a distance. The background laughter of the men around them faded into nothing; it was as though the two of them were alone together. He nodded his head in her direction and placed his Stetson on his head.

The gesture was old-school, and although she knew he didn't mean anything by it, there was something about it that just…*did* it for her.

"Now we'll see some action!"

Althea broke eye contact with Nate, her heartbeat thumping hard in reaction to the silent, swift, but heated exchange.

"In what way?" she asked, forcing a smile to her lips.

The foreman nodded his head in Nate's direction. "Nate. Used to break broncos back in the day. Even did some riding when he was younger. Taming a stallion ain't nothing for him!"

The surprise must have shown on her face as the foreman laughed.

"Riding, as in bull riding?"

"Yep, did pretty damn good too," he said. "Did it for a couple of years. Made a helluva lot of money, that's for sure. Enough to help the boys expand the ranch. They all did what they had to do to see the Wyoming Wilde successful. They're good men." The last words were said in a gruff tone of voice, but the pride on the older man's face was obvious.

Althea turned with him and watched Nate's long-legged stride take him toward the fenced-off corral where the last defeated cowboy endured the laughter from the others as he hopped over the fence, playing along good-naturedly with the ribbing he received.

Folding her arms along the rails she watched his long stride take him toward the wild-eyed stallion, unaware of the look on her face, one that made a thoughtful smile cross the foreman's face as she pressed her body closer to watch the action.

Chapter 7

Nate ran a quick hand down the horse's back and slapped it lightly on the butt. The horse lifted its head and neighed loudly, yet turned a docile nuzzle into Nate's hand, accepting the food he'd withdrawn from his pocket.

He turned around, facing the men who stood around clapping, nodding his head toward them. "And that, boys…is how you tame a horse."

He accepted the pats on the back and congratulations, and allowed one of his men to approach the newly tamed Appalachian and lead it away.

He removed his Stetson and swiped a hand over his sweaty forehead while his eyes scanned over the small throng of men, seeking out Althea.

He'd known she'd been watching him while he tamed the horse, and although for his own safety and from experience he knew his mind had to be on the horse, he'd been just as aware of her dark gaze on him and caught himself fighting the urge to return her look.

Now, as he stood in the middle of the corral, many of the men beginning to disperse and attend to their duties, their gazes locked.

He ran his gaze over her deliberately as he walked toward her, sliding his eyes over her from the top of her head, where she was wearing her typical ponytail, over the thick bangs feathering across her wide forehead, down over the thick parka she wore and over her long legs encased in jeans.

She took a step back, away from her position near the fence, and turned as though to go.

"Ms. Dayton, I need to have a word with you," he called out before she could make good on her escape.

She paused but kept her back to him. Her body was stiff, her back straight and head held high.

For a moment he thought she'd defy him. That she'd pretend as though she hadn't heard him speak.

He jumped over the fence, walked closer and waited.

After long moments she finally turned and faced him.

Although she kept her face neutral, showing no trace of expression, in her dark eyes he saw a glimmer of fear mixed with an awareness of him, and something more. Something that defied explanation.

The same mix he'd seen the first time he'd met her in the stable. That same one that made his body tighten and harden to marble whenever he thought of her, was anywhere near her.

The same one that made him to want to grab her, haul her hot little body close and kiss her until she was senseless and neither one of them knew their own names.

He inhaled, his nostrils flaring. He could *smell* her.

He took several steps closer until he stood less than a foot away from her, glaring down at her, his mood darkening.

He stood so close Althea could smell his unique scent wash over her. She closed her eyes briefly, tried to get herself together, and reminded herself over and over in her mind that there was nothing he could do to her, there was nothing he could say or do to push her buttons.

She shoved away the persistent images that had plagued her with irritating regularity of the way he *could* push her buttons. The hot, sweet, erotic ways she knew that he could.

She opened her eyes and ran her gaze over him.

She looked up the length of his long, long legs. The muscles in his thighs bulged as though fighting the confines of his jeans. She studiously avoided glancing at the other bulge and continued her perusal up his body.

He'd taken off his coat, despite the chilly weather, and was only wearing a soft chambray cotton shirt that molded the thick muscles of his chest. Slowly Althea raised her eyes to meet his. Although he'd placed the Stetson back on his head and his face was partially obscured, she felt the intensity of his unwavering, penetrating stare.

She blamed the chilly wind for the way her nipples constricted against her bra and the slew of goose bumps that broke across her skin.

When she'd watched him taming the stallion, her

heart had pounded ruthlessly against her chest, her eyes glued to his every move. The way he approached and ultimately tamed the wild horse was nothing short of beautiful. Man and beast facing off, both determined to conquer the other.

As the others had shouted encouragement from the sidelines, Althea had been silent, her eyes glued to Nate's big body as he refused to allow the large, muscular stallion to throw him.

Riding the wildly bucking horse, his body jerked in every direction, yet his hold on the animal remained firm, the battle of wills one he was determined to win, until finally the horse had been the one to give, the man the victor. A wide grin had split across his sensual mouth.

And then his eyes had sought hers. The smile had dipped from his sensual mouth, but not the intensity of its effect on her.

Althea shuddered at the memory.

He stepped closer.

At that moment, the wind picked up again. With it, his distinctive scent assaulted her, making her draw in a gasping breath. It was the type of smell that no cologne manufacturer could ever hope to duplicate.

He was the epitome of man. And everything she should be afraid of.

Yet as she stood before him as he silently made his assessment of her, not speaking, he was everything she'd been yearning for in ways she wasn't able to…no, not *willing* to think about.

She *absolutely* didn't need any more complications in her life. God knew she didn't.

She had learned to live day to day, take life as it came. And this man...this man was the definition of complication if she ever saw it.

But that part of her—that deeply feminine part she'd kept locked away—didn't care about any of that. Her body reacted as though from a script. Again.

Her nipples tightened beneath her bra and her stomach rolled, hollowing out as though she were on a roller coaster. She took an involuntary step back.

Swallowing deeply, she fought to get her mind...her body, under control, determined not to allow this man to affect her.

"What did you need to speak to me about, Mr. Wilde?" she asked, forcing the words out of a mouth gone dry.

What was going on inside her mind? Nate wondered as he locked gazes with her, her expression unreadable.

No matter how neutral she kept her features, he'd seen the telltale sign of her reaction to him when her dark honey skin flushed, her dark eyes going over him before she'd glanced away, drew in a breath.

He ran his eyes over her hair, secured in a messy ponytail, the thick fringe of bangs across her brows, and barely checked himself from reaching out to finger her hair, test to see if the strands were as soft as they looked.

"I finished my chores...sir," she finally said, her voice husky. She cleared her throat. "What...what else do you want from me?" she finished, a hint of defiance lighting her almond-shaped eyes.

With her question, both his body and mind went

into full-on battle. His mind told him that what he felt whenever he was around her didn't make any damn sense, and the fact that she was on his mind twenty-four/seven even when she was nowhere near him was something he needed to walk away from while he still could.

But his body told him it was time to show her, in detail, exactly what he wanted from her.

His gaze stole over her cheeks, which were stained with a hint of a flush, to her eyes, which were focused on his mouth.

His body won.

Without giving a damn if anyone was around to see them, he placed a hand at the indenture of her waist, tunneled one hand through the soft, wet tendrils of hair at the base of her neck and tugged her body until it was flush with his.

Before she could catalog in her mind the clarity of his intent, he'd brought his mouth down and covered hers.

On cue Althea's eyes slowly shut and one short, hitching breath of air escaped before she gave in to his embrace.

The feel of his mouth on hers was electric as his lips brushed back and forth against hers in a feathery caress. The intimacy was so unexpected a moan escaped.

At her moan, he pressed her mouth open, widening it, demanding entry before pressing his tongue deep inside. He easily maneuvered past the barrier of her teeth, sweeping once, twice, within the cavern of her mouth, before retreating.

Tilting her head, his tongue again swept inside her

mouth, in and out, smoothly, rocking inside her in lazy sweeps.

"Ahhh…" she moaned into his mouth, bringing her hands between them and grasping the front of his shirt, clutching the soft cotton in her hands and holding on for dear life against his silent yet deadly assault on her senses.

He kissed her like a starving man. Licking and stabbing his tongue against hers.

His mouth greedily took hers, alternating between soft, biting caresses and long sweeps of his tongue. Consuming her mouth until she felt dizzy, her mind and body spinning, going up in flames.

Althea moaned, clutched his shirt and stood on tiptoe, lost in the sensual assault, pressing herself close to him, the heat from his big body surrounding her, overwhelming her.

He broke the kiss and she whimpered, desperately clutching at him her eyes flew open and sought his.

"As far as what I want," Nate said, his breathing harsh as he dragged his mouth away from Althea's lips, her soft, tempting curves. Her eyes were cast low, her lips puffy and swollen from his kiss, the soft, sensual stamp of need on her face making his shaft strain against his fly as she stared up at him.

He fought like hell the temptation to haul her back against his body, fought the need to pick her up and go caveman on her, throw her over his shoulder and find the nearest place to lay her down, finish what they'd started.

Reining in his body, the unexpected devastation of a

kiss that only added fodder to his overactive libido, he forced out the words he needed to say. Words he knew would throw salt on his game, but he had no choice.

What the woman was doing to him, the way she had his mind all twisted, thoughts of her never far away, images of stroking into her sweet body... He had to put an end to this, before it was too late.

The effect she had on him, with just one look, one kiss, was one he didn't want or need. He hardened his mind, refused to be taken in by her sweet mouth, her soft voice, her ringing laugh. He refused to be taken in by her. She was no different from any other woman. There was always an angle.

"I want to make sure you realize that I've been watching you. I don't know what your game is, why you're here, what your angle is." He brought his mouth down, the last words fanning the hair at her temples, "But unlike my brothers and the rest of the men around here, I'm not easily taken in by a pretty face and hot body. You'll do the same work as all the others, or get the hell off my ranch."

Her eyes widened and then quickly narrowed, the stamp of sensuality evaporating so quickly it was as though it was never there.

Surprising him with her strength, she shoved at his chest, pushing him away. Caught off-guard, Nate stumbled before he regained his footing.

She stepped away, wiping the back of her hand over her mouth, a look of disgust replacing the soft sensual one that had been there moments ago.

His gaze centered on the soft line of her jaw that was now tightened in anger.

"I don't know who did this to you," she spat out and stopped, took a breath and stepped back, farther away from him. "Who made you think all women are the same, that we're out to get something or get over."

She angrily spun away, her body jerky, as though she couldn't stand to look at him anymore, but then spun back.

"But let me just tell *you* something, Mr. Wilde, whoever it was, that's not me. And I'll be damned if I'll allow you to make me your punching bag. Been there, done that. And believe me that will never, *ever* happen again."

Chapter 8

"How's Althea doing? I haven't seen much of her lately. Any reason for that, Nate?"

The question held an underlying accusation, one Nate was waiting to hear from Lilly.

He gave her credit. He'd been expecting to be called on the carpet way before now. Lilly was like a mother to him and his brothers. And she was originally from the south.

The combination was a one-two punch, and she never had a problem speaking her mind to any of them.

He turned away from staring out of the large bay window in the kitchen to face her.

He crossed his arms across his chest, watching as she finished chopping vegetables and scraped them into the large, simpering stockpot on the stove.

"I haven't given the woman a thought, Miss Lilly.

Left that up to my brothers. I wouldn't be the one to ask how she's doing," he lied glibly.

After his last confrontation with her, she had been on his mind so much that it had played havoc with his concentration, making it damn near impossible for him to rid the image of her shy, hesitant smile, or the way her lips, soft, sweet, had feathered across his.

Or the feeling in his gut when he remembered the way her face had fallen, her liquid brown eyes had held a wealth of emotion for that brief moment—lust, sadness, and finally anger, all because of him.

He blew out a breath and grabbed the back of his shoulder with a hand, the knot of tension building since their encounter days ago.

With a large wooden spoon in hand, Lilly slowly stirred the contents of the large stockpot, not saying a word, leaving him to his own ruminations.

Not only was Nate aware of how Althea was "doing," he knew *what* the woman was doing, at any given time. He'd made sure of it.

But when he'd seen Holt with her, although he'd told himself good riddance, unbidden, unreasonable jealousy reared. He knew Holt. Knew that his brother would find it damn impossible to *not* try and charm the woman right out of her panties. The man was a legend around the local town of Landers.

But he had no right to say anything, had given his brother the go-ahead to keep her out of his way.

When he'd spied the two of them near the stables, he'd watched as Holt had helped her into the saddle, his hand hovering too damn close to her curvy backside for Nate's comfort level. Realizing the unreasonable jealousy he felt, he'd angrily spun around to leave. Before he could she turned and caught his eyes.

The smile on her face, one that caught his breath, slowly slipped away when they made eye contact, and Nate could practically feel the tension oozing from her slight body.

The two of them had stared at one another for so long, it had taken Holt's presence to break them out of their mutual absorption in each other.

Holt's wide, easy grin split his face as he caught sight of Nate, and with his eyes on Nate's, had grasped her around the waist and pulled her from the horse, keeping his arms around her for longer than necessary. Nate had turned on his heels, abruptly leaving the pair without a word. He'd heard his irritating brother's deep bark of laughter trail behind him on the wind.

"If you have something to say, Miss Lilly, say it," Nate bit out, irritated more with himself than with her. Over the last few days he'd sunk to new levels, asking the workers about Althea, where she was and the job she was doing, not trusting himself to ask his brothers, fearing what he'd do to one of them, particularly Holt, depending on the answer.

Lilly continued stirring the pot as though she didn't hear him. Finally she placed the spoon on the trivet in the center of the oven, wiped her hands down her faded apron and faced Nate.

"Don't you think it's time you let that go?"

"What's that got to do with Althea? One has nothing to do with the other."

Nate didn't pretend ignorance. He knew what she was referring to. Or who. Angela, the woman he was engaged to two years ago, the reason he no longer allowed women on the ranch.

"It has everything and nothing to do with her," she replied, softly.

"You can't have it both ways, Miss Lilly."

"Don't get smart, boy. You know what I mean," she shot back, lifting the spoon from the trivet and waving it in his direction.

"It has everything to do with you and what you've become since you allowed that…woman," she started, on a roll now, hands on hips squaring off against him. "Since you allowed Angela to get you all twisted into knots. Let what she did to you sour you on women…on life, love."

"I don't have time for this, I—"

"Don't you walk away from me, Nathan Hunter Wilde."

Although she spoke in a low voice, her tone stopped Nate dead in his tracks. And the fact that she said his full name. He knew better than to ignore her when she was in full-on rant mode.

"I raised you and I know the kind of man you are. You're a strong man. You got hurt, and you've got your pride. I understand that. Okay, deal with it. Move on, or be this way for the rest of your life. It's your decision. But taking out on all women what one did is not only stupid but it's getting old, Nate. Real old. It's time to move on. Put on your big-boy shorts and deal with it."

Nate felt a smile threaten to break free, despite his irritation at Lilly's interference into his life and his overall sour mood.

That was all she'd said, but it had been enough.

So much so that Nate now found himself doing something he never thought he would, purposely seeking out Althea.

Ignoring the tension between them, the reason for it, wasn't going to make it go away. The sooner he faced her, this…whatever it was between them…the sooner he could get her out of his mind, his thoughts, once and for all.

"Are you busy?"

Nathan Wilde's deep voice broke into Althea's thoughts.

Spinning around she came face-to-face with the man who had been playing havoc with her mind during the day, her body at night as he crept his way into her dreams regularly since the day they met.

"I…I didn't know you were around," she lied, swallowing down the melon-size ball of anxiety. Although she hadn't seen him, as usual she'd been aware of him the minute he came within a fifty-foot radius of her.

It was late afternoon, and after finishing work, she'd been at loose ends and had wandered over to watch the men break in a new steer. She glanced at him from the corner of her eye.

Standing so close to Nathan Wilde, his scent, his heady unique smell reached out and strangled her. Taking a step back, she put as much distance between them as she could without it being too noticeable, her hip bumping against the wood railing.

Her gaze went over him. Dressed in what she'd come to think of as typical cowboy wear, he wore a fleece-lined sheepskin jacket, worn jeans and equally worn cowboy boots. But on him, the traditional fare was anything but.

The jeans hugged his thick, muscular legs, the jacket, unzipped, revealed a plaid shirt, the top buttons undone and a sprinkling of dark hair at the V peeking through.

When he stopped in front of her he removed the ever-present Stetson he wore, revealing a face that again made her breath catch at the back of her throat.

"Ms. Dayton?" He broke into her thoughts, and Althea fought against the heat she felt raising to her cheeks. Standing there just staring at the man, he probably thought she was a few bricks shy of a load.

"Althea…please call me Althea, Mr. Wilde," she murmured, extending an olive branch. When he didn't return the favor, inviting her to call him by his first name, she pulled herself upright, straightening her shoulders.

She reached a hand up to try and push a strand of hair back into her ponytail, the biting wind blowing the errant strands across her cheeks.

She raised startled eyes in his direction when he reached a gloved hand out and pushed the strand back up into her hair. Moistening her bottom lip with her tongue, she thanked him, her voice hoarse.

"I'm going out to the south pasture. Wondered if you'd be interested in going along?"

Althea tried, but knew she failed, to prevent the surprise from showing. For him to actually invite her to be with him was no less than startling. She was still reeling from their last encounter.

Which was why she'd gone out of her way to avoid any interaction or contact with him the few times she'd seen him over the past few days. And he seemed just as determined to avoid her.

Over the days, although the ranch was large, and there was work to be done literally from sunup to sundown, from baling hay, moving cattle, tending the various acres and a myriad of other duties, this was the first time she'd seen him since the time he'd accused her of…God only knew what the man had been accusing her of…in nearly a week.

She glanced up at Nate's scowling face, the way his thick, smooth brows met in the middle, studying her as though she were an object under his own personal microscope.

"Well? Are you ready? Can you come with me?"

"Ready for what?"

Althea felt her heart kick against her ribs at the unmistakable light that entered his light brown eyes, his casual but thorough perusal of her…before his gaze settled on her lips.

"Ready to come with me."

Dear God.

Did he have to phrase it in that way? With that deep, sexy voice of his?

Her glance ran over his face, down the line of his

strong neck, to the pulse that beat at the hollow of his throat before trailing back up to meet his gaze.

Again his eyes were on her mouth. She blew out a small breath, remembering the smell of his minty breath mingling with hers, the way his mouth slanted over hers, the brief but incredibly erotic taste of his lips on hers.

Her tongue snaked out to swipe across the bottom rim.

Although he'd answered in a neutral tone, the underlying thread of sexual tension racing between them gave his answer an *entirely* different meaning.

Nate stared down at the woman in front of him. She'd asked him what he was ready for.

The immediate answer to her question that came to mind was one he knew would get him in trouble if he dared utter it.

He found his gaze settling on her lips, the sexy curve of her bottom rim, the slight bow at the corners, before he dragged his eyes back to hers.

He recalled the feel of her lips brushing against his. The shy way her small tongue darted out and tangled with his for their brief yet erotically charged kiss, the kiss, the feel of her body on his replaying in his mind over and over throughout the last week, so much so that he woke up nightly, sweat pouring, his own hand on his shaft, wishing it were her instead who fisted him.

"Ready to come with me." He forced the answer past clenched jaws.

Her brow furrowed, her mouth pursed, a question forming. Before she could speak, he finished, "I heard you've been getting a real good sample of life around here. Thought you'd be interested in going out with me to one of the lower pastures to witness a live birth. The hands just called the vet, she's about to give birth any moment. The vet could always use a couple of extra pair of hands. It's pretty bloody, though. And probably a pretty difficult birth. The cow mated with one of our larger bulls, and the calf is going to be a big one. Don't know if you'd be interested…" He allowed the question to dangle, stopping. He felt like a damn adolescent asking a girl he was crushing on for a first date.

"Yes, I'd…I'd love to," she answered, a small smile lifting the corners of her mouth. When her face lit up, he nodded shortly, ignoring the kick of his heart at the way the smile transformed her face.

"Don't know how well you ride, so we'll take my truck…"

"Oh, I know how to ride. I love to ride!"

"Two lessons with my brother and you're a regular equestrian," he stated more than asked, realizing too late how telling his admission was.

After the first lesson Holt had given her, Nate had made it his business to learn of any subsequent lessons, not trusting his brother alone with the woman. He'd told himself it was because he didn't want Holt taking advantage of her as an employee, yet knew that wasn't the case.

"How'd you know about the second lesson?" she asked, a curious look crossing her face, pulling a frown between her brows.

Nate ran his fingers across her brows and removed the frown. When he saw her draw in a breath, he allowed his fingers to stay for a fraction longer before he pulled away.

"I know everything that goes on, on my ranch."

Without another word he cupped her beneath the elbow and steered her toward the stables, her body tucked close to his.

Chapter 9

Just as Nate had predicted, the birth was long, bloody and difficult to watch.

And Althea seemed to love every minute of it.

The cow, average in size, had already mated before Nate had purchased it, to a much larger European breed. Something he and his brothers never did with their own cattle, as the calf was less likely to survive and many times the cow died as well during the difficult birth.

Throughout the birthing, although his focus had been on the health of the cow and her calf, Nate's attention had been drawn, countless times, to Althea. He'd watched her with what he couldn't deny was growing fascination and attraction.

Without hesitancy she'd helped, no matter what was needed. Although he and Dr. Crandall were there, along with an additional ranch hand, the difficulty of the birth added tension and stress to the situation, and every hand was needed.

But more than anything, he'd found his gaze drawn to her face, the expressions alternating between awe and amazement, to sympathy for the cow's pain, particularly when a tough contraction hit the animal.

At one point their gazes had connected, and to his amazement he'd seen the sheen of tears in her dark brown eyes before she hastily glanced away.

Without being asked, she stooped down near the cow's head, running a shaky hand over its face, whispering soothing words to the animal, much as she had with the horse the first day he'd met her.

When she began to hum softly, the animal's cries lessened, its ears flickering, the fear in its eyes diminishing. Nathan felt a part of his heart stir, unlike anything he'd ever felt before.

He'd watched and assisted in more births than he could count. And although this one was by no means an easy birth, the vet having to reach inside the cow to reposition the calf more than once, it wasn't the worst he'd ever witnessed.

Yet Althea's empathetic response to the animal's stress made it almost feel as though he were experiencing it for the first time, along with her.

When the calf finally made its appearance, his attention went first to Althea, and he saw the relieved smile cross her mouth, the impractical tears that ran unchecked down her smooth cheeks.

She glanced up at him at the same moment. He felt

an answering smile, unknown to him, lift one corner of his mouth as the two of them shared the moment together.

When he bent to assist the vet, pulling the calf the last few inches from its mother's womb, from his side vision he saw Althea rise.

"You did it, girl." As the cow stumbled to its feet, she brushed a hand over its neck, moving out of the way to allow it stand.

"You're a mama now, Bessie, congratulations!" She laughed, sniffing away at the tears.

"Bessie?" he asked, the corners of his mouth twitching.

She turned toward him and gave a little shrug of her shoulders, the grin still in place. "I don't know...the name seems to fit. Besides, all new mommies deserve a name."

"And you have experience in that?"

She tilted her head, frowning, the remnants of her smile still in place. "In cow naming? Can't say that I have. I've named a few dogs in my time. A few cats as well. I even named a chipmunk once." The humor lurking in her eyes brightened. She shrugged one shoulder again. "I can't say that I've ever named a cow before, though."

Nate nodded his head, going along with her, as though it was perfectly normal to name a chipmunk. "And what did you name the chipmunk?"

"Alvin, of course," Althea replied, straight-faced.

After her lame quip, he groaned and a raspy chuckle escaped from his sensual lips, the sound rusty, as though it had been a while since he'd laughed. Dr. Crandall chose that moment to glance at both of them briefly, his head moving from one to the other, a smile coming to his tired face before he turned back to the calf.

"Funny woman. You got jokes, huh?"

Althea laughed outright, her mood brightening.

She didn't know if it was watching the amazing birth, or the fact that she'd helped in some small way in bringing a life into the world…or the fact that she was with Nate Wilde, but suddenly she felt lighter… less burdened.

"I've been known to, once or twice." She paused, her glance gliding over Nate's face, noticing the smile that lingered around his sensual, full lips making her heart skip a beat.

"You…you have a nice smile, Mr. Wilde." She hadn't known she was going to say the words even as they flew out of her mouth. Or what possessed her to say them in the first place.

When she saw his smile drop away, Althea wished she could retract her comment. One day spent together didn't mean the man liked her, or had even changed his opinion of her.

"Nate," he said, after a brief pause. "Call me Nate," he finished, his voice gruff.

The small concession he gave shouldn't have made her heartbeat quicken, shouldn't have meant a thing to Althea.

But it did.

"Well, if you two are done with the introductions…

Miss Bessie and Bessie Jr. did quite well, I'd have to say!" The veterinarian broke in, dragging Nate's attention reluctantly away from Althea.

"Yeah, that they did, Dr. Crandall."

Dr. Crandall had been with the ranch from as early as Nate could remember, dating back to his foster father's early days when he'd first bought the land. He'd been the first and only vet that Clint Wilde had hired to help him with his then-struggling ranch. As the vet had been new to the area, as well as being the first and only black veterinarian to set up shop in Landers, Wyoming, it had been a slow and difficult building of his practice.

But Clint Wilde hadn't cared about the color of Dr. Crandall's skin, had only cared that he could help him take care of the animals' medical needs on his struggling ranch.

From there the two men had forged a friendship that lasted Clint's lifetime. When Clint Wilde had died seven years ago, although there were plenty of other vets in the area the Wilde men could have hired, there was no thought to replace Doc Crandall. He, like all the others who were a part of the ranch, was family.

Nate helped Dr. Crandall to his feet. For a moment, as he watched the older man struggle to his feet, he wondered how long it would be before he retired. He handed him his cane.

As though reading Nate's thoughts, Dr. Crandall looked across at him, a tired smile creasing his lined cheeks, and slapped him on the back.

Hard.

Nate barely stopped from pitching forward at the hearty slap, and caught the twinkle in the older man's fading dark brown eyes.

"I ain't dead yet, son…plenty of time for me to keep on practicing. Besides, soon, Yasmine will be joining me," he said, pride shining in his eyes as he mentioned his daughter. He glanced around. "Think you all can handle the cleanup, son?" he asked, and Nate nodded.

"Yes sir, we can handle the rest. Marc here will help," he said, nodding toward the cowboy who'd been helping with the birthing.

"Good enough." He glanced down at the watch on his wrist. "Been a long day, time for me to head on back home. The wife and I are expecting Yasmine to call and let us know when her flight is in."

"She's coming back soon, then?" Nate asked as he walked alongside Dr. Crandall, subtly keeping his hand near the old man's back in case he needed assistance.

From his side vision he saw Althea watching him and Dr. Crandall, the look of longing on her face surprising him. She quickly glanced away, but not before he saw the shimmer in her dark eyes.

He turned away reluctantly.

They'd worked side by side over the last few hours, and the more he was around her, the more he wanted to know about her.

The more he wanted to dig into her history and discover what secrets her dark eyes held hidden and locked away.

"Not for another couple of months. I got her ticket a bit early is all," the vet replied. Nate felt the love and pride the old man had for his only daughter, who'd recently completed veterinary school and after a year doing a residency in Cheyenne and was returning to help her father in his clinic.

Before they left, Dr. Crandall turned toward Althea. "You are welcome at any time, to help me in any way whenever I come by, miss. You are an amazing young woman."

She simply nodded her head, thanking him silently, but Nate saw the way the vet's casual words affected her.

"I'll be back, and we can head out."

Left alone with the ranch hand, Althea stood out of the man's way as he took care of the duties of cleaning up, watching with a smile on her face as the mother, once the afterbirth had been expelled, had lain back down, her calf already rooting around, searching for milk.

By the time Nate had returned, another ranch hand had come to help. His glance fell to Althea. Noting the tired look on her face, he motioned for her to come with him.

"You look tired. I think it's time we called it a night."

She smiled at him, replying, "I could say the same of you," as she walked toward him. He waited until she was by his side and extended his hand.

"I think it's time we both called it a night."

He saw the flicker of indecision enter her eyes. He waited while she made the decision. The knowledge hovered between the two of them, that her taking his hand was her acceptance of what had been brewing between the two of them since their first meeting.

It was an acknowledgment of what was to come.

Taking the decision away from her, he grasped her by the hand. He briefly gave his men final instructions and turned with her to leave the stable.

The time for waiting was over.

Chapter 10

Both Nate and Althea were wrapped up in their own thoughts, and the drive back was made in silence, the tension in the cab of his truck thick, heady.

After he'd reached his hand out for her to take, his hot glance sliding over her, Althea's body had reacted as though he'd touched her.

When he'd taken the decision away from her and taken her hand in his big warm one, wrapping it around her suddenly cold fingers, a part of her had been relieved.

She knew what it meant, taking his hand. As simple as it was, she knew.

A glance into his eyes and she'd seen them darken, his hot gaze trailing over her face, down the line of her throat, back up to her mouth. Yes, she knew. He wanted her.

And God help her, she wanted him just as bad.

Piggybacking her self-admission, fear kicked in

immediately. Fear of what it meant if she agreed, through silent admission, to what his eyes promised he wanted from her.

The need to flee came quickly, nearly overwhelming in its intensity.

This fear wasn't the same as those of the past, the ones that told her danger was coming her way, that Reggie had found her again.

No. This feeling, this *need* to run had nothing to do with fear that she would be harmed in a physical way.

This fear was that she wanted…*yearned,* for him to do what his eyes promised he wanted to do to her.

Every decadent carnal thing…and more.

Her fear had everything to do with the fact that she would gladly turn her body over to him and allow him to do those things to her.

In every way.

She adjusted her body, turned slightly so that she could sneak a glance at him from beneath lowered lids.

His hair, closely cropped in the back, was longer on top, long enough to form a slight curl, the strands so dark and silky-looking her fingers itched to reach out and touch them.

His nose was strongly chiseled and dominated his angular face. A slight stubble covered his lean cheeks and strong squared chin, not enough to hurt…just enough to provide a pleasurable sensation if he were to…kiss her.

She forced her mind away from the thought of where she wanted to feel that scratchy kiss on her body.

Although there was no smile on his face, strong lines

scored either side of his sensual mouth, as though at one time he'd smiled, and smiled often.

Althea wondered what…or who, had taken the smile away.

With a sigh, she looked away.

Nate felt an odd apprehension settle in his gut as he walked Althea to the cottage, one that was foreign to him.

The drive had taken only fifteen minutes, yet it felt as though it had been hours. He'd felt her gaze on him several times but had resisted the urge to return her look. It was hard enough for him driving with her so close to him, without pulling over and finishing what they'd started from the first moment they'd met.

He'd had to rethink his opinion of her over the course of the evening. Truth told, he'd had a subtle shift in thinking regarding her over the last week.

His reaction to her from the beginning should have clued him in. But he'd fought against it, fought like hell against the chemistry between them, fought to keep her at a distance both physically and mentally.

For all the good it had done. He'd never felt the pull he felt toward her with any other woman. No woman had ever taken him from red-hot anger and irritation to rock-hard excitement, all within minutes, like Althea did.

Not even Angela, the woman he'd been engaged to.

Yet there was something else about her that troubled him. Aspects of her didn't jibe with who she presented herself to be; a nomad, a woman who called any place she hung up her hat home.

He glanced down at her, the top of her head barely reaching him at chest level, again reaching out to take her hand, this time leaving the decision to her. He wanted her to be a willing participant this time, wanted her acceptance of what the day had been leading to. This time, Nate waited.

When she placed her hand in his, his heart thumped hard against his chest. There was a measure of trust in her placing her hand in his, he felt it. One that told him it wasn't something she did easily.

Together they walked the remaining distance, her small hand nestled within his much larger one. When they reached the front door, she fidgeted in one of the pockets and withdrew the house key.

Before turning to unlock the door, she turned to him.

This time her face was in full view, the light from the porch casting an amber glow across her beautiful, somber features.

"Thank you for today," she said, after her fumbling fingers managed to unlock the door. "I mean, for letting me help. That was one of the most amazing—"

Althea turned to face Nate, her heart banging around so loudly in her chest she knew he had to hear it.

She stopped speaking midsentence, her breath catching at the back of her throat.

As she glanced up into his face, the lighting on the porch created an odd intimacy, one that seemed to shroud them in a world of their own.

Shadowing his handsome face, the light fell at an angle that highlighted the piercing way he was looking at her, the glint in his eyes one of raw masculine lust that was so palpable that Althea swallowed past the lump in her throat.

The look in his eyes made her heart pound and caused a rush of liquid heat to trickle into her panties.

"I...I think I'd better go. Than-thank you, uh, again," she stammered, backing into the cottage.

Before she could think to try and close the door, he had placed one big foot inside, pushing the door farther open.

Advancing into the cottage, he didn't bother to turn and close it, simply kicked it closed with the heel of his booted foot.

"I think we need to talk," he finally said. Although his voice was a low rumble and it was in direct contrast to the blazing look in his eyes. It was a look that said he wanted to do much, much more than talk.

Biting at the bottom rim of her lip, Althea couldn't force a word out of her mouth to save her life. Clearing her throat several times, she gave up and simply nodded her head in agreement.

Moving aside, she allowed him to enter the cottage.

Chapter 11

There was no way in hell he was leaving her, not at least without tasting her lips, feeling her sweet curves against his.

The entire day, thoughts of what lay hidden beneath the bulky parka she wore had played hell with his libido. The fact that he'd been able to wait this long had proved nothing short of a miracle.

He glanced around, surprised that he didn't feel the surge of anger he normally experienced when entering the cottage.

He'd built the house for Angela, thinking they'd make it their home, where they'd raise their children. When she'd turned her back on it…on him, he hadn't set foot back inside since. He would have torn the damn thing down if his brothers hadn't stopped him, reminding him of the hard work they'd all done to have it built.

Now, as he followed Althea farther inside, his mind

wasn't anywhere on the woman from his past, instead fully concentrating on the one in front of him, his gaze fixated on the sexy sway of her hips as she turned on lights.

She came to a stop inside the kitchen area, turned around to face him. Her nervousness was obvious. She couldn't even make eye contact with him, looking at everything and everywhere except him.

He leaned against the tall column that separated the kitchen from the living area and crossed his arms over his chest.

"Can I…can I get you something?"

"If you have tea that would be great. Of the sweet variety. Unsweetened tea is for wimps."

His answer surprised a laugh out of her, making her relax. Good. He wanted to put her at ease. Wanted her to give in to him. Wanted her to want him as much as he wanted her.

And just like the horses he tamed, ones that had been hurt and didn't give their trust easily, all it took was the right touch. He was ready to touch her in all the right places, but first he had to gain her trust.

He was up for the challenge.

She removed her jacket and placed it over a chair before kicking off her sneakers. Without glancing at him, she swiftly removed her socks at well, tucking them inside her shoes. He hid his surprise when he saw her toes, the nails painted bright pink, emerge from the thick white socks.

She caught him looking at her and smiled slightly. "I like being comfortable whenever I'm home. It's been a while since I've felt this way," she said, and lifted one shoulder in an offhand shrug that was so casually sexy, Nate felt his cock thump against his jeans in reaction.

She took him from zero to one twenty in three seconds flat. Without even trying, he thought.

Damn.

He pushed away from the wall and walked into the kitchen toward her. Pulling out one of the high-backed bar stools, he folded his long frame into it. Bustling around the small kitchen, she removed a tin and withdrew two tea bags, and when the timer chimed on the microwave took out the mugs and dumped the bags inside.

"I hope cookies are okay? I made them myself," she said, pulling out several large, thick cookies from a can and placing them on a plate in front of him.

He eyed them, gingerly picking up one of the oddly shaped cookies.

"What? You're afraid to taste my cookies?"

Nate glanced up at her and caught the gleam of humor in her eyes. His eyes on hers, he lifted one from the plate. "No, I'm not afraid of tasting your…cookies," he replied, taking a bite, his eyes on hers as he chewed.

Her eyes widened, the humor evaporating from them, a molten awareness taking its place.

Althea felt her mouth go completely dry as she watched his full, sensual lips open, his white teeth flash as he bit down into the cookie. When his tongue came out and caught a crumb, she thought she'd melt right on the spot.

The man was lethal to her senses.

Her eyes were fixated on the line of his strong jaw

as he methodically chewed the cookie, the muscles in his neck standing out in stark relief as he swallowed, working the bite down his throat.

No man should be able to eat cookies and turn a woman on at the same time.

After he finished chewing the cookie he nodded his head. "You were right, they are good," he said, surprise in his voice.

Relaxing as the sensual tension eased a bit, she lifted a cookie, bit into it and chewed. "You sound surprised."

"I am, a bit."

"Why?"

He looked her over, his eyes narrowing. "Somehow I didn't see you as the type."

"The type?"

"To be able to bake cookies like this. But maybe that's the end of your cooking abilities?" he asked more than stated, leaving the question open.

"Actually I know my way around the kitchen." She volunteered the information. "Over the last two years, I've learned to cook and have served more meals than I had in my lifetime."

"You didn't know how before?" he probed, and Althea stopped short, realizing how revealing her response had been.

She shrugged. "Let's just say I've added a bit of knowledge to my core base and leave it at that."

"Why don't we take this over to the sofa and sit down," he said, indicating the tea.

With a nod she agreed, and followed him over to the sitting area.

Instead of choosing to sit on the smaller, more intimate love seat, she chose instead the roomier sofa, seeking even on a subconscious level to put some space between them.

As she sat down, she placed the tea on the small table placed in front of the couch. Although he gave her space, his big body seemed to take up *way* too much room on the sofa. Althea subtly shifted her body, moving farther down. From her peripheral vision, she caught the knowing look cross his handsome face.

As though he was more than aware of how he affected her.

"What brought you to the ranch, Althea?" he asked after several moments of companionable silence.

Althea placed the mug down on the table in front of her and turned toward him, tugging at her upper lip in indecision.

She didn't want the ease of the moment to end. Didn't want to think about her past, or what brought her here, or to any of the many places she'd lived over the last couple of years.

Although she'd come to have a measure of trust with the men who ran the Wyoming Wilde, she was nowhere near ready…or willing…to talk about her past in its entirety to Nate.

Yet as she looked at him, there was a part of her that wanted to tell him. Wanted to unload at least some of the burden she'd carried for two years.

She inhaled a slow, steady breath and began.

"I grew up with my father, just the two of us, from the time I was only five. I don't really remember my mother too much. Just small bits of memory scattered here and there, times when she would read me a story or she and Dad would tuck me in at night. She had cancer and was always sickly. She died when I was young."

As she spoke, he placed his mug on the table next to hers and sat back, his attention solely on her.

"It was me and my dad for as long as I remember," she began, an unknowing smile tugging the corner of her mouth upward as she thought of her father. "We did everything and tried everything together," she said and laughed. "Including horses. Dad had always wanted a horse when he was a kid. He grew up in what he called 'the country,'" she said and laughed lightly. "But his family didn't have a lot, and definitely didn't have enough money to feed a horse. Even so, Daddy always wanted one, and every day after school when he was younger, he'd go to one of their neighbor's houses and in exchange for feeding the animals, he was allowed to ride the horses."

Althea went on to tell him how she and her father had been inseparable, and how her father had been the one to teach her to ride a horse and on her twelfth birthday he'd surprised her with a small palomino of her own.

"No wonder you seemed so natural riding with Holt," he commented, and paused. "Why did you act as though you hadn't ridden before?" Although the question was asked casually, Althea felt on the spot, it sobered her, reminded her that she couldn't become too relaxed around him.

She had evaded the truth, disguised who she was for a long time. Every small thing she considered, and although she had done it out of self-preservation, she wondered, briefly, what he would think if he knew the

entire truth about who she was, where she came from…
why she could never go back.

"I never said I couldn't," she hedged. "It's just been a
while. Thought I could use a refresher course and when
your brother offered, I agreed. That's all."

His piercing stare made her uncomfortable and she
dropped her eyes, a finger reaching out to toy with the
rim of her mug before bringing it to her mouth.

"And your father…" He allowed the question to
dangle.

He saw the hesitation, as though she were carefully
weighing her words, trying to determine how much to
tell him. How much she trusted him.

"Before I was born, he traveled a bit. He said he
always wanted to travel more, but when I came along
he settled down and raised me. Like I said, it was only
the two of us for most of my life."

Nate nodded his head, encouraging her to continue.

"My father was…an entrepreneur of sorts. He dabbled
in a few different areas; he created patents for a few
products that did well. The money he made he invested
in the stock market. Another one of his other interests.
With the growth of his business he took on a partner."
Althea stopped, drew in a breath.

"Actually Reg—he—was more like a mentee, to
Daddy."

Nate caught the correction, knew that for whatever
reason, she didn't want to tell him the man's name. He
filed the knowledge in his mind to think about later.

"Although he'd worked for a well-known brokerage
firm for a few years, he wanted to work with my father.

A lot of people saw my father as a pioneer in the investment field."

Nate remained silent, not wanting to interrupt her.

In the short amount of time he'd been around her, he'd come to the conclusion that whatever secrets she held close were ones she wouldn't give up easily.

Over the course of the day, he'd also come to realize that he wanted to get past the wall she had erected, past the mask she showed to the world. He wanted to be the one she trusted.

As soon as the thought entered his mind, he was brought up short.

Damn.

He didn't know when it had begun to mean so much to him, that she trust him, open up and share herself with him. Didn't know when she had come to mean so much to him.

It was a line he'd crossed, but now that he had, he knew there was no turning back.

She mattered more to him in the weeks since she'd come to the ranch than Angela, the woman he was engaged to and knew for over a year, ever had.

The thought was sobering.

"My…my father died a few years ago in an accident," she said, bringing him out of his own startling discovery. Her tone was matter-of-fact, as though she were telling him the weather forecast instead of about her father's death.

Until he looked down at her hands.

She held them clenched, tight, in her lap, rubbing the thumb of one hand over and over against the palm of the other.

He casually reached over and placed his hand over hers, soothing the nervous gesture, silently giving her the support she obviously needed.

"When he died, I…left." She opened her mouth to speak and closed it, inhaling a deep breath, glancing away from him she finished in a voice so low he had to strain to hear the words. "There was nothing for me in D.C. anymore."

"I'm sorry," he replied, although he knew the words were inadequate. He also knew there was more to her father's death.

She glanced up at him. In the depth of her dark eyes was such raw emotion, Nate felt his heart slam hard against his chest in reaction to her obvious pain and chose not to probe further.

She looked away, but not before he saw the glimmer of tears in her eyes.

Nate had lost his own father at an early age, yet the memory of how he'd felt when the sheriff had come knocking on their front door, letting him and his aunt know his father was killed in an accident, was one he never forgot.

His hand tightened on hers, tugging at her until she faced him.

Without a word he pulled her close, brought her head to nestle on his chest.

Her soft cries tore at his heart, but he continued to stroke her hair, allowing her to cry softly, without interruption from him.

He lifted one of her clenched fists that rested on his chest, opened it and brought it to his mouth, and softly kissed the center.

She pulled away, softly sniffing, and sat back against the cushion, yet kept her body close to his.

She wiped at her eyes with the back of her hand and offered him a trembling smile that didn't quite reach her eyes.

"And here I am. Traveling like Daddy always said he'd wanted to do, exploring…doing the things Daddy and I would have done, together. One day. At least that was our plan."

He wanted like hell for her to continue, but knew the moment had passed. There was so much more, he knew, than she had told him. Gaps that he desperately wanted filled in.

But it was enough. For now.

He still held on to her hand. When she tugged away from his grasp, he allowed her the distance, looking her over. She seemed so small sitting there.

Fragile, delicate.

And the day had taken its toll on her. The T-shirt she wore clung to body, molding the sensual curve of her small yet firmly round breasts. Despite her overall disheveled look, her fragile beauty was palpable, and drew him to her.

Her vulnerability made Nate want to wrap her in his arms and promise her that whatever secrets she held, whatever caused the emotion to darken her eyes, would be safe with him.

She was safe with him.

Whatever reason she had for leading the life she did, wandering from place to place, with no roots to tie her in one place for long, he longed for her to feel safe with him.

"Thank you," he said finally. Simply.

She held his gaze for a moment, and then nodded her head, silently.

His glance fell to her hands again. Now she held both of them in her lap, palms up, again running her thumb over the palm of the other, massaging them. Something she did when lost in thought.

He lifted one, turned it over in his, running the tips of his fingers over her palm. Despite evidence that she worked hard, there was a hint of softness, one that hinted that she hadn't always had to work the way she did.

He raised his eyes and found her somber, liquid gaze on his. His eyes went to her mouth.

Her perfect bow of a mouth.

The upper rim had a slight protrusion, exactly in the center; a slight puffy swell that he'd felt the first time he'd kissed her.

He brought one finger up to trace over it, slowly. When her eyes fluttered shut he brought his head down and brushed his lips over her entire mouth, his tongue darting over the puckering with light, teasing flicks. She moaned softly, in a whispery sound of need.

He pulled away and brought her palm up to his mouth, running his tongue over the raised calluses, in tribute to whatever had made her run, work any and every job she could in order to survive.

To whatever had brought her to him.

Althea drew in a shuddering breath when she felt the featherlike strokes of his tongue against her skin.

When his tongue followed the path up her wrist, kissing the length of her arm, her body melted, liquid heat easing from her, and every nerve ending in her body went up in flames.

The caresses were soft and light, fleeting, yet were the most sensual thing a man had ever done to her.

He licked the same path down again, ending at her fingers, drawing each digit deeply into his mouth to dart and play, swirling his tongue over the pads of her fingers before releasing each one.

She opened eyes drowsy with need to meet his heated gaze.

When he drew her closer, unresisting, she went into his arms.

His light brown eyes darkened, filling with lustful, decadent intent.

With a harsh groan he cupped the back of her head, brought her close to his mouth and claimed her lips again.

This time he was methodical; slow and easy, he made love to her mouth.

Swiping his tongue against her lips, slicking the seam of her lips in a lazy back-and-forth, seesawing motion, he encouraged her to open for him. Althea eagerly obliged, opening her mouth, giving over to his silent edict, and immediately she felt his slick tongue sweep inside.

The first stroke of his tongue, boldly entering her mouth, was like molten lava to her senses. Pervasive and deep.

With a deep, harsh groan he brought her body against his until nothing separated them but their clothing.

So close Althea felt the hard, stiff ridge of his shaft intimately against her stomach.

She moaned, her eyes closing tight, reveling in the feel of his erection and his hard, sensual mouth against hers.

The kiss was crazy, wild and unlike anything she'd ever experienced.

He didn't just kiss her. He consumed her in long sweeping motions with his tongue, he licked, stroked… made love to her mouth with hot, carnal ferocity.

Mewling softly, Althea lifted her arms and placed them around his neck, seeking…needing to be as close to him as she could, to give in to what had been building for weeks, grinding her body against his, caught up in the sensual web they'd mutually created.

Her hunger for him, his warmth, his touch, rose sharp and engulfed her in flames the longer they kissed and caressed to near incendiary heat.

Not thinking of right or wrong, Althea completely gave herself over to the moment, over to Nate.

The moment she wrapped her arms around him, her soft hands tunneling through the hair at the back of his head, tugging him closer to her much smaller frame, Nate's body hardened to painful readiness.

For most of the day he'd been in a steady state of semiarousal. Working so close to her, side-by-side, it had been nothing short of miraculous that he'd been able to keep his mind on the job of calving.

Impatient to feel her soft skin against his, her round, plump breasts naked against his chest, her long legs wrapped around his waist…his body firmly imbedded, deep, deep inside her sweetness, he palmed both of her soft round globes in his hands and brought her into his lap, lifting her enough so she straddled her legs on either side of his on the sofa.

She moaned when his hands tunneled beneath her shirt and skimmed over her unbearably soft skin, down her waist, until he reached the top band of her jeans.

Without losing contact with her mouth, her sweet, decadent mouth, he brought his hands out of her jeans and back up her waist until he felt the thin band on the back of her bra. Deftly, he unsnapped it and impatiently shoved the bra down her body until it lay around her waist before shoving it completely from her body.

Lifting her shirt, he stared down at her unbound breasts, his heart beating in a hard, unrelenting rhythm simply from seeing her this way.

"No, don't hide from me," he said, his breath coming out harshly when she placed her hands over her freed breasts. "Please don't hide from me. God, you're beautiful." His last words were torn from him.

He placed his hands beneath the thin T-shirt, skimming them up the length of her stomach until he reached the undersides of her firm, round breasts.

Gently he cupped them, their soft weight filling his hands to perfection. He ran a thumb over each tightly drawn nipple and watched in fascination when they spiked, growing long, hard against his fingers.

His eyes sought hers.

There was lust and desire in them, yet there was also a thread of fear, one that made Nate pause.

"I'm sorry," he said, his voice low, deep. "I'll go slow. I promise. You don't have to fear anything with me, Althea. I'll never hurt you." The promise was made with sincerity.

The depth of his sincerity, although real, shook Nate. Brought his impatience to feel her body against his to a momentary standstill.

The truth was, as much as he wanted to strip her bear, imbed himself deep inside her heat, he would rather cut out his own heart than be the one responsible for hurting her.

Her slumberous eyes held a bright sheen, a vulnerability that tugged at his heart and made him want to find the bastard responsible for putting it there. From what she'd said, his instincts told him the man who worked with her father had something to do with whatever had made her run, whatever had caused the fear lurking in her eyes.

Beyond her father's death, there was another reason behind her vulnerability.

He withdrew his hand and thumbed away the tears that had escaped and now trickled down her soft cheeks, landing at the corners of her bow-shaped lips.

He bent down, captured the tears in his mouth, and softly kissed her lips.

"All I'm asking is that you trust me. I won't hurt you."

While he had been determined not to get his heart involved with another woman, somehow this woman, a woman who still held her secrets guarded closely, had managed to pierce a chink in his emotional armor.

If his brothers or Lilly knew, he'd never hear the end of it.

"I won't do anything to you that you don't want done. I promise you," he said, staring into her eyes. Unable to resist, he kissed her soft lips again before he raised his head. Reading the hesitancy in her eyes, he continued. "Anytime you want to stop, just say the word, okay?"

For long moments she stared at him, her eyes searching his, for what Nate didn't know. He waited.

He'd wait as long as it took.

The strength of the self-admission shook him to the core.

As she stared up at him, again he was struck by her fragile beauty.

Her large eyes scanned his face, searching for what Nate didn't know. Her tongue snaked past her kiss-swollen lips to lick the full bottom rim, and he bit back a groan of need.

But it was her eyes that did it to him, forced him to still the crazy need in him, the need to pick her up, carry her to the floor and make love to her until neither one of them could think straight, until all fear and hesitancy vanished as though it never had been.

That same wild need he felt, he saw reflected in her eyes, behind the hesitancy.

When she finally nodded her head, relief swept over him, and his body reacted to the simple declaration of trust.

"Yes."

The one word was all he needed to hear.

Nate closed his eyes briefly, opened them and kept his gaze on hers. Placing his hands on either side of her face, he leaned down and kissed her, his hands gliding down to reach under her shirt and drag it up her body, the ends bunched in his fists as he stared.

Keeping his eyes on hers, he captured one of her nipples, suckled on it, pulling it deeply into his mouth until it spiked again, long and hard, bumping softly against the roof of his mouth.

She arched herself fully into his mouth, called his name softly in erotic entreaty. Nate growled against her plump breast, pulling her pliant body so tight against his he felt every soft curve of her body.

As his mouth caressed his breasts, he picked her up, cradled her in his arms and walked toward the fireplace, their mouths still linked.

Once there, he placed her down on the plush brown rug, and after giving her one final kiss, one last caress, he reluctantly broke away and rose, kicked off his boots and socks, keeping his attention on hers the entire time.

"Wha…what are you going to do to me?"

At her words he paused with his hand on the front snap of his jeans.

"I'm going to do whatever you want me to do."

He slowly unsnapped his jeans.

"I'm going to taste and caress every inch of your body."

He drew the zipper down and began to peel his jeans down his legs.

"I'm going to lavish…worship—" He kneeled down, placed a kiss on her mouth, "Every delicious—" he rained kisses down her chin, her throat "—part of you," he finished huskily, and drew her turgid nipple deeply into his mouth, then slowly released it.

His gaze sought hers. "If you let me."

"If you let me…"

Althea's eyes fluttered closed, a moan of acceptance tumbling from her mouth.

At the current state she was in, Althea doubted there was anything she wouldn't allow him to do to her.

She drew in a deep, shaky breath as she lay on the rug, watching Nate as he removed his clothes, slowly unveiling his body to her, first casting his shirt over his head and with careless disregard, tossing it on the floor, revealing his thick, hard chest to her hungry gaze.

She ran her eyes up the length of him, starting at his feet, past thick thighs that bulged with muscles, her heart stammering against her chest when her gaze lit on his shaft.

His thumbs hooked into his shorts and his shaft sprang free. Thick, hard, erect, it lay against the tightly packed muscles of his abdomen, the mushroom cap hitting him well above his navel.

Swallowing past the constriction in her throat, her eyes traveled over his rock-hard chest to the small nipples that were a shade darker than his dark caramel skin, until she met his eyes.

His body was a work of art, the picture of raw, masculine perfection.

When her eyes met his, the look in them, an indescribable mix of lust and need, caused an answering need in her to rise, forcing her to clench her legs together as she felt her own essence trickle down and pool into her panties.

Nate's nostrils flared, his shaft growing harder when he saw her reaction to him, the way her slumberous eyes unashamedly gazed at every part of him, her chest rising and falling in shallow breaths.

She in turn made his blood boil, the picture of pure

sensuality as she lay on the rug, half-clothed, her hair a messy tumble around her shoulders.

Her nipples, dark, were silhouetted against her T-shirt, the fat nipples protruding, pushing against the thin fabric.

His eyes dropped to her jeans. The top buttons were unfastened and the scrap of pink lace of her panties hid that part of her he desperately needed to get at now.

Keeping his gaze on hers, his hand snaked down and grasped his shaft, rock-hard and ready. Joining her on the thick rug, he covered her mouth with his.

Tugging and pulling at the upper rim, he sucked her lip deep inside his mouth, running his tongue over the erotic little puffy flesh in the center until he felt it tighten.

He released her mouth, his breathing harsh. She moaned, a helpless sound of distress at the disconnect.

Placing his forehead against hers, he fought to control his body, whispering, hoarsely. "Before we go any further, I have to make sure this is what you want, Althea. If we don't stop now, I don't think I can."

He drew back, moving far enough away that he could see her face, searching her eyes.

In them was the same wild need. A need that acknowledged what he felt, that she too didn't want to stop. The fire building between them no longer one she could or wanted to contain.

With that, he went to work on her clothes.

At last she lay nearly naked on the rug, her pretty full breasts bared to him, her long legs stretched out on the floor, one leg bent, one hand covering her panties as though to shield herself from him.

Nate brushed her hand away, replaced it with his, running his hand over the short, curly sprigs of hair covering her mound.

"Don't hide yourself from me," he murmured. Leaning down, he replaced his hand with his mouth, kissing her through the silky material.

Her body vaulted sharply off the rug, arching until her breasts nearly met her bent knee. He fingered aside the elastic along the leg of her panties, worked a finger inside and rubbed against her core.

"Nate...no, what—" she panted, before throwing her head back, moaning sharply when he placed both hands beneath her knees, pushed her legs far apart and pressed aside her panties to place hot, languid, intimate kisses between her slickening folds.

She clutched at him, placing both hands at the back of his head, trying to push him away, but he continued his deadly assault, his caresses alternating between long, easy glides of his tongue to sharp, flickering darts.

Her head tossed on the floor as she issued sexy little cries of distress, her fingers gripping his forearms so tightly he knew he'd have marks in the morning, but he didn't care.

Her mewling cries of feminine distress grew, her body tightening, a fine tremor invading her limbs. A glance upward, and he saw her head as it tossed on the floor, her long lashes fanning her cheeks as she kept her eyes closed, accepting his oral loving.

The sudden feel of his velvet smooth tongue against the tightening bud of her clit, and Althea's body no longer belonged to her. She cried out, her body completely bowing, the release so close she felt tears prick the backs of her eyes.

When he covered her entire mound with his mouth and kissed her, she let go.

Her body fell back as she gave in to the mind-blowing release, screaming as she came.

By the time her release was complete, when the violent tremors had left her body, she felt him centered between her opened legs.

Taking deep, panting breaths in an effort to calm her racing heart, she opened her eyes and met Nate's hot gaze, the look in them sending a fresh wave of tremors throughout her body.

He rose, lifted her from the floor and carried her through the cottage toward the bed.

Chapter 12

Whan Althea felt the bulbous end of his shaft press against her slick folds, a semblance of normalcy returned.

And with it a dash of unwanted but needed reality; she wasn't on birth control.

"Stop," she murmured as she felt his shaft begin to press past her swollen lips.

"Baby...what?" he panted, his arms braced on either side of her body. A glance into his eyes showed the strain and effort it took for him to even speak.

She closed her eyes and bit at her bottom lip.

"I...I'm not on anything," she said, swallowing down the sting of disappointment. "Protection, I mean. I'm not on the Pill."

She felt his chest rise and fall against hers but didn't venture a look up at him. When she felt his body shift slightly away, she opened her eyes to see him opening the side drawer of the night table.

After a few moments of impatient fumbling, he came back to her, a small foil package in his hands, his light brown eyes staring down at her, a gleam of masculine triumph within their depths.

"I suppose it's the smart thing to do, keeping protection so handy," she murmured, pulled out of the moment slightly, not sure if she should be jealous that there were condoms available on standby.

He leaned down and kissed her softly on the lips. "I've never used these. They were just put there by one of my brothers, probably trying to be funny."

The explanation, although succinct, was strangely satisfying.

When he brought their mouths into close contact, slanting his mouth over hers and pressing his slick tongue inside, Althea forgot all about the odd jealousy, giving herself over to the moment, the two of them, his big body draped over hers, their bodies, hot, pressed close.

Placing his hands beneath the bend of her knees, he opened her body wide, sliding between her bent knees; she felt the knob of his shaft against her mound. With featherlike strokes he rubbed it against her moist lips, nudging them apart, asking for entry.

With a moan she pressed against him, wrapping her legs around his waist, silently given her permission.

The minute he began to feed her his shaft, her body began to shiver uncontrollably. Her hands came out to clamp tightly on his powerful forearms, stilling his invasion.

"Wait…wait," she panted, swallowing deep. "It's been a long time…oh God," she moaned when she felt his finger come out and rub her clitoris over and over until her cream eased down, saturating his finger.

"I don't know how much longer I can wait, Althea." His voice was a coarse rumble against her ear.

She moaned, tossing her head on the pillow, and he slowly began to penetrate her.

"I'll go easy on you, baby."

The erotic promise made her body tremble. She bit her bottom lip to prevent the cry when he grabbed her hips, slowly feeding her more of his turgid shaft. One final thrust and he was deep inside her. Her breath came out in hitching gasps as her body adjusted to his hardness.

He swallowed her cry as his hands reached around and lifted her bottom high, bringing her hips into tight, hot alignment with his.

"Nate…" she cried softly, as he began the slow drag and pull inside her body.

Her soft whispers and cries, the sight of her eyes closed, mouth partially opened as he pressed inside her body, made Nate's balls tighten and his cock grow harder inside her slick heat.

With a grunt, he lifted her higher, her body coming completely off the bed, and rocked steadily into her, over and over until her moans grew to cries of feminine surrender as he steadily plunged inside her sweet heat.

On and on he rocked into her, their bodies slapping against each other, her soft cries the only sounds in the room.

Glancing down at her past the haze of lust and sweat, her smooth brown body glistening with their combined moisture as she ground against him, his thrusts became deeper, so deep her head kept grazing against the headboard.

Deftly he eased her body down, never losing connection with her, their bodies in perfect symphony as he powered inside of her.

He wanted to string out the pleasure, make her as hot for him as he was for her, but the feel of her walls milking his shaft was his undoing.

And when he felt her small hands reach down and lightly grasp his sac, it was over.

Her light touch made his body tighten, sweat fall from his face down to her body.

He pumped inside of her in tight rhythmic thrusts, no longer able to maintain control. He felt her orgasm sweep over her. Her body jerked as she screamed, her legs tightening on his waist urging him to his own release.

Nate waited as long as he could, gritting his teeth as her walls clenched his shaft, until with a tight groan he let go.

From a distance he heard her cry out again, and grabbing her by the hips he flipped her over, angling his shaft back inside of her and thrusting.

With three more pumps deep inside her he felt his orgasm jet from his body as he reared back, bellowing out his release, the muscles in his neck corded, veins pulsing as he finally gave in to the mind-blowing release.

He slumped down on top of her. Sweat mingling, their bodies clung together. Reluctantly he pulled out of her, turned her so that she faced away from him, her bottom nestled against his groin.

He felt her stir after long moments, and brought her around to face him.

"That was…that was amazing," she whispered, almost shyly. "Thank you," she said softly and immediately blushed.

When his cock stirred again, he lifted her leg, laying it over his, repositioning her body.

"We're not done, yet," he said, smiling in satisfaction when her eyes widened, her lips forming a perfect O.

Chapter 13

As Reggie's fingers flew across one of the library's keyboards, he was thankful for the computer and technology classes he'd been forced to take while serving time, years ago.

Although he was quite sure the administrators over at the education system at the federal pen had no idea he'd taken the skills he'd learned in computer operations and become so proficient at hacking into main systems. Something else he'd learned while serving time, though not from the instructor.

Never being one to allow an opportunity to pass by, he'd discovered a fellow inmate with a very marketable skill: hacking computer systems.

Even though Reggie found the man distasteful, using his skills for petty crimes, he'd latched on to him and sucked him dry of all the information he could. Adept at learning, after his stint it hadn't taken him long before he'd also used the skill to alter his record.

During his eighteen-month stay at the pen for embezzling, he'd used the remainder of the time to reinvent himself. Voraciously reading everything he could get his hands on, from business skills to high society, an idea began to form.

It had sprung forth during black history month, of all times.

He giggled lightly as he continued his search.

He'd read about a successful African-American man named Charles Dayton, his story fascinating Reggie, in the lifestyles section of the newspaper. He'd been a pioneer in investment banking and also one of the first African Americans to excel as he had in the field.

There, a plan had begun to hatch. Particularly when he saw the man had a beautiful and single daughter. He had taken his time, learning everything he could about Charles Dayton and his daughter, Althea.

Learned that she was the closest person to him; whenever he saw one of them in a news clipping, he saw the other.

They were two regular peas in a pod, he thought with a sneer.

Not that any of that had mattered.

As his fingers flew across the keyboard he laughed lightly.

She could have been buck-toothed and married and none of it would have mattered, he thought, a chuckle escaping.

There. He had her!

Hmm…so, she wasn't quite as smart as she thought she was.

She'd gone to Wyoming…he squinted his eyes, scanning the screen. Landers, Wyoming, not Montana, as she'd wanted him to think.

It was all a part of her game. A game of cat and mouse.

In her arrogance she didn't realize he knew more about her than she thought he did.

When she left, she'd started using her mother's maiden name, as though that would hide her from him.

He'd come so close that last time to getting her back. So close to getting her to come back, marry him, sign the documents he needed to give him access to her father's fortune.

He sat back in the chair, his thin lips pursed, a small smile on his face. The smile dropped when he remembered the first time he'd found her after she'd left him. Hiding behind a counter, cowering from him in that cheap motel.

He'd lost it. Dragging her from behind the counter, his anger had gotten the best of him, and in the ensuing fight, he'd banged her head against the counter. The memory of the deep gash and gushing blood from the cut filled him with satisfaction.

She shouldn't have hidden from him.

He loved her. Besides the money, he loved her. She was his. The sooner she realized that, the sooner they could go on with their lives and end this craziness.

Now she was using her mother's middle name, Dayton, on the fake identification she'd gotten. But it was her. He could tell from the picture—although grainy, it was her.

He ran his finger over the screen, over the blurry image.

He'd been careful at first, had hired a few…old acquaintances to find her. His lips curled in disgust. All they'd managed to do was scare her, make her more vigilant and harder to find the next time.

But now he trusted no one. He knew it was up to him to find her, bring her back home, and everything would return to normal.

In the afterglow of perfect lovemaking, Althea's body felt like butter. Liquid. Boneless.

Land o' lakes all the way, she thought, a smile flickering across her generous mouth at her mental quip.

"Am I to assume that I'm the cause for this smile?"

Althea opened her eyes and turned. Shifting her body until she was facing Nate, her smile grew wider.

"Hmm. Maybe," she said, and giggled softly when he playfully tickled her, finally crying uncle.

"Okay…yes, yes, I give." She laughed softly. "Yes, you are." She felt a sudden wave of shyness when she caught the way his light-colored eyes seemed to darken, his gaze going to her mouth. One long finger reached out to trace down the side of her face.

She turned her head away.

He caught her by the chin, raised her face toward him, forcing her to look at him.

"Why do you do that?" he asked, frowning.

Althea wanted to reach up and smooth away the

frown that creased his brows, but stopped herself. The instinct seemed so intimate, a thing lovers did, touching freely. Although they'd spent the night making love, she didn't fool herself into thinking it was anything but what it was; two people acting on a one-time, mutual desire.

Although incredible, unlike anything she'd felt before, that's *all* it had been.

A one-time thing.

A blush rose to her cheeks as she remembered the many and varied ways they'd touched and caressed each other throughout the long night and early morning. The way his steady strokes and hot kisses made her feel.

How she'd wakened once to find him covering her, his shaft pressing intimately against her; how readily she opened herself to him, eagerly reaching out to him.

Yet for all of that, as intense, passionate, wild and sensual as their loving had been, she still felt unsure of him. Of her own feelings.

"Do what?" she finally asked, allowing him to tilt her chin up, her eyes meeting his.

"Tuck your head away when I try and touch your face."

Her hand reached up and touched the scar that was a constant reminder of what had happened the last time she hadn't ducked in time.

His frown increased, his eyes narrowed. Moving her hand out of the way, he moved her hair aside. Reaching a big, muscled arm over her, he turned on the small bedside lamp, bathing the room in a light glow.

When he bent down and softly kissed the scar, that part of her that she'd held back for so long beat at her to be released, demanded she give in to what her heart was telling her was real.

But her mind? Her mind fought back just as hard, stubbornly telling her that it couldn't be. Not so soon...

"Whenever you're ready to tell me the reason for this," he said, switching off the light and bringing her body in front of hers, her bottom nestled firmly against his groin, her back blanketed by his wide chest. "Know that I'll do whatever it takes to make sure you're never hurt again."

She simply nodded her head, battling against the tears burning the back of her throat.

Even as Althea lay in front of him, her body curved intimately against his with a casual, natural intimacy that belied their brief acquaintance, Nate wondered when it happened. When had the tables turned, and what started out as a need to satiate himself with her and get her out of his system once and for all, turned into something more.

Damn.

As she lay in front of him, Nate felt the tension creep into her body, tension that hadn't been there moments before as they made love.

Even as he fought against what was happening, fought against feelings he didn't want to have, with a woman he knew held deep secrets, he found himself wanting to break through her barriers, her defences.

It had been when she'd first run, after she'd realized what Reggie had done. The horror of that day still lingered in her mind.

She'd been going through the last of her father's things, clearing out boxes. She hadn't realized she'd overlooked a small fire box. With a frown on her face, she'd realized it was locked, and tried to remember where or if she knew of a key. Her instincts had led her to the cheap ceramic box her father had always kept, from as long as she could remember, hunting inside the box for the key.

Lifting the box, she opened it, and nestled inside was a small key. Taking the key, she'd walked over to her bed with the fire box in hand and sat down, placing the key into the lock

A perfect fit.

An "awareness" came over her. One that told her that whatever was inside the box would unlock part of the mystery surrounding her father's death. Told her father had committed suicide on his boat, Althea had felt a wealth of conflicting emotions, from doubt and grief, to anger. Anger directed at both herself and her father. Anger at her father for leaving her, and herself for somehow missing signs that would have prevented his suicide.

She'd allowed Reggie to speak on her father's behalf to investors as well as see to the running of his business, after Reggie told her that in the weeks preceding his death, her father had decided to make him a full partner, showing her the document her father had signed stating that fact. Too caught up in grief to do much else, she'd easily agreed, not asking any questions, thankful that he'd been there to help her.

Carefully, she'd opened the box. Inside were several sheets of paper, stapled together. With a frown she'd unfurled them and scanned the words. As she read the hastily written words in her father's scrolling hand, her stomach had dropped, nausea filling her gut.

It appeared as though her father had been approached to invest in a new communications company that on paper appeared promising, ready to go global. There were several documents showing the communication with them, all looking as though they'd come from her father's email address.

With a frown, Althea read over the official-looking documents. Her father, from the communication, had been pumping a significant amount of money into the startup business. So much money that Althea wondered how he could afford to invest so heavily.

Behind one of the documents was a DVD, covered in a hard plastic case. She lifted it from within the box.

She stood and walked over to her laptop, and popped the disk inside the drive.

It was an audio recording. The first sound of her father's voice brought an unexpected wave of emotion and tears.

She sat up straight, carefully listening when she heard Reggie's voice as well.

The two of them had been arguing, her father's voice deep baritone, although not raised, filled with anger as he confronted Reggie.

"What the hell were you thinking? I trusted you, damn it! Brought you in when no one else would have you. Not only do I find out you're not who you pretended to be, I find out you've been stealing from me, too? I ought to—"

"*Ought to what, old man?*" Reggie broke in. His voice was hard, unyielding.

Reggie's tone was so completely unlike the cultured one she was accustomed to hearing that Althea's eyes widened in shock, her heart pounding even more against her ribcage.

"*I'll tell you what you're going to do. What you're going to do is go along with this. As you can see, to all intents and purposes, your name is the one on the documents, your signature. No one will believe you had nothing to do with this. I've got this covered on all angles.*"

"*Covered on all angles? Have you lost your mind? You can't steal from my clients and think—*"

"*If you play this right, just chill the hell out and let this play out, no one will know. And in the end, we all stand to make a hell of a lot of money. If you don't...*" Reggie's voice trailed off.

"*But why, Reggie? Why in the name of God would you do this? I've spent years building this company. Years of hard work, years of sacrifice. And I'll be damned if you destroy everything I've done.*"

Althea heard a scornful laugh from Reggie. "*Damn man, stop with all the theatrics. No one will know the difference. By the time your precious clients know, they'll all be richer for it. They'll be glad I...you...did it.*"

"*That's not the point, you son of a bitch. The point is you had no right to steal from them. And what if this company of yours goes belly up? What then? What will you tell the people you stole from?*"

Again Althea heard Reggie's high-pitched laugh.

"Well, if that happens, that's a bridge you're going to have to cross. And if the company goes belly up?" Althea could see him in her mind, shrugging one rail-thin shoulder in disregard of what he'd done to her father.

"Whether they make money or not, I've already made mine. I'll be long gone before the shit hits the fan," he said, his high-pitched laugh ringing out again.

With her fists clenched, Althea listened. Before she could hear her father's reply, her cat, meowing loudly, caught her attention.

In agitation the cat tangled itself around her legs, her cries becoming louder, so loud Althea's heart began to pound. Althea looked to the cat, and toward the door. The animal always did that whenever Reggie was around; it had never had a fondness for him.

Without pause, she quickly shut the computer down and ran to her bed, throwing the documents back inside the box and shoving it back where she'd gotten it from.

Moments later Reggie came inside her bedroom, a look of concern plastered on his face.

"Hey baby, I was calling you, didn't you hear me?" Reggie's dark eyes scanned over her as she sat on the edge of the bed.

She sent a fervent prayer to God that he hadn't seen the box she'd shoved underneath it.

When his gaze went to her hand where she clutched the key to the lockbox, she casually smiled and stood. She'd moved to her dresser, where she pretended to take something out, putting the key inside before turning back to face him.

She ran a tired hand through her hair, forcing a smile onto her face, her heart now racing so hard she was afraid he could hear it from across the room.

The look on his face as his dark eyes went from her to the dresser and back sent a wave of fear to course over her.

With her newfound knowledge of him, in his eyes she also saw proof that he had been the one behind her father's death.

A frown creased Nate's forehead as he felt the tremor go through her body. This time it wasn't from his touch.

Nate brought her into his arms, her back to his chest, and pulled her close before lightly resting his head against hers.

Chapter 14

Althea's laughter rang out when the cows continued to crowd in on her as she tried to cut the large bale of hay. She glanced over at one of the ranch hands standing nearby cutting his own bale, and he gave a shrug of his shoulders.

"Goes with the territory, I guess," she said, laughing, and the foreman, along with several of the other men, laughed along with her.

She'd spent the morning with Nate's foreman, cutting the string that tied the large bales of hay. She'd then helped to break up the large, round bales and spread them so the cows could graze.

After she fed the first pasture and the hungry animals had all gathered, bumping against her in their eagerness for chow time, she'd soon learned to move fast around the hungry cows.

After breaking up the bales, by hand or pitchfork, the

cows were more often than not too impatient to wait and eagerly tried to get to the food before dinner was ready to be served, to her amusement.

She wiped away at the beads of sweat that peppered her forehead, looking up into the midday sun.

She'd woken after the amazing night she'd spent with Nate and found herself alone in the bed.

Althea had raised frantic eyes to her alarm clock, and when she'd noted it was several hours past the time she normally woke, she'd jumped from the bed and quickly showered and dressed.

She'd turned to leave the bedroom when she spotted a slip of paper that had fallen on the floor, next to the side of the bed where he'd slept.

After bending down to retrieve the note she rose, reading it as she did.

In a bold, masculine sprawl was a short, to-the-point message: *Didn't want to wake you. Sleep in. Don't worry about working today.—Nate*

And that was it. And he'd signed his name, as though she wouldn't be able to figure out it was from him.

Really, what had she expected? A love note with flowers and hearts drawn over the scrap of paper?

She laughed softly and shook her head. "Not hardly."

Nonetheless, she'd tucked the note into one of the back pockets of her jeans, grabbed a bagel and carton of juice from the refrigerator, and after locking up, left the cottage, pondering the short, cryptic note.

Did he think that because she'd slept with him she wanted...expected...special consideration?

Scratch that, sleeping was the least of their activities

throughout the long night, Althea thought, feeling heat flood her face as she thought of the many, many things they'd done that hadn't included sleep.

It had been so long since she'd felt like she had last night, so long since she'd enjoyed being with a man, making love, no other thoughts invading her mind. It had been even longer since she'd allow herself to just let go and enjoy.

After finding the foreman she'd found out that Nate and his brothers had gone out to one of the northern pastures to move cattle. One part of her had been disappointed, but the other part had been relieved, not sure how to face him "the morning after."

She'd found Lilly in the kitchen after following the guidance of one of the ranch hands. Thinking she'd be trailing after the same man who she'd been reporting to for her daily chores, he'd told her she was to go to the main house instead.

Lilly had then informed her that Nate had given instructions for her to take care of Althea, for her to help in the kitchen if she wanted.

Although the older woman had given her the information in a matter-of-fact tone, Althea had picked up on the side glances she'd cast her way as she swiftly whipped the cake batter and poured it into the greased baking pan, along with the glimmer of curiosity in her dark brown eyes.

"Take care of me?"

Lilly dusted her hands down the sides of her ample, apron-covered hips and lifted the large pan to place the cake inside the oversize oven.

She'd then turned to Althea. Although she gave

Althea a considering look, she simply nodded her head. "That about sums it up."

At that, Althea felt the tips of her ears burn. Mumbling a thank-you, she'd left the house and sought out the foreman. She'd become used to working the ranch, and although she enjoyed Lilly's company, she preferred working outside with the others, as she'd done the entire time she'd lived there.

Now, as she finished with the last bale, she reached up again to wipe the sweat away from her forehead, a satisfied smile on her face.

As usual, although the work had been hard, it had been immensely satisfying. Glancing around at the others as they worked, Althea was struck by the sense of family she felt around the men. Although most had been with the ranch for years, even those who were recent employees exhibited the same sense of pride and commitment to the ranch as those who'd worked there much longer.

Which said a lot for the men who owned and operated the ranch. Nate and his brothers were a breed apart.

She'd learned they had come together on the ranch as young boys, that the owner, Clint Wilde, had been a loner, living out on the ranch alone with the exception of those who'd worked for him.

Clint had never married, as far as the others knew, and when asked by the director of a local boys' home if he was interested in a new program that would place the boys in area homes in exchange for them working and learning about ranching, the gruff rancher had agreed.

Eventually he'd adopted them. After he died, he left

the entire two hundred acres, along with everything else he had, to his adopted sons.

She glanced around again at the working men.

Realizing they were all caught up in work, she was about to pick up the bale of hay when several of the hungry animals began to crowd her again.

Laughing along with the others she hopped away, avoiding their hungry cries and nudges. She quickly broke up the hay, her laughter ringing out along with the others.

Nate observed Althea with the cows, her antics trying to dodge the hungry animals making everyone around her laugh, including himself.

He hadn't thought she'd be awake, much less working, after the night they'd shared.

He'd woken before dawn and had turned to her, ready to pick up where they'd left off, before realizing she still slept.

He'd trailed his hands over her body, moving the sheet they'd used to cover themselves away so that he could cup one of her breasts lightly in his palm. She'd softly sighed and moved closer to him, her firm bottom nestling snugly against his groin.

After spending an entire night making love to her, it still hadn't been enough. He'd moved his other hand around so that he cupped both breasts, lightly toying with her nipples until they spiked against his hand. He held back a groan.

Even in sleep she responded to him.

The faint shadows beneath her long lashes prevented him from waking her and starting over, making love to her until neither one of them knew where one left off and the other began. Damn.

With a deep sigh, he'd carefully untangled himself from her, and deciding not to wake her with a shower, dressed.

Walking slowly back toward the bed, he'd stared down at her, one side of his mouth hitching upward. She'd turned in her sleep after he'd gotten up and now held the pillow he'd laid his head on hugged against her, her face buried against it.

Reluctantly he'd turned away, found a piece of paper and pen in the nightstand drawer and written her a note. Before he could change his mind, he turned and left.

Her laughter brought him back to the present. As she hopped around the nudging cows, his eyes narrowed to slits when he noticed he wasn't the only one entranced with her. Several of his men had stopped working just to watch her antics, grins of appreciation on all their faces.

When his foreman gave several of the men watching stern looks, telling them without words to keep working, the knot of jealousy loosened and he relaxed, the scowl on his face easing away as he leaned on the railing to continue his perusal of her.

He was so caught up enjoying the show he hadn't realized his brothers had joined him until Holt slapped him on the back.

"Thought we'd find you here."

"Meaning?" he scowled, pulling his gaze away from her.

Holt shrugged a big shoulder. "No hidden meaning,

big brother…heard Althea was here, ergo…" He allowed the sentence to dangle.

Nate squashed the desire to knock the obnoxious grin from Holt's face and instead deftly changed the subject.

"Everything set for roundup this weekend?" he asked, turning to Shilah.

"Yeah, got most of the men ready," he said, and for a short time the men discussed the upcoming event until again Althea drew Nate's attention away from his brothers.

"So…when are you going to tell us what's really going on between you two?"

Before he could speak, Shilah, normally the less… intrusive of the two, piped in, "Give him a break, Holt. The man's got a right to his privacy. None of our business what, or if, anything's going on between him and Althea." It was more the humor lurking than what he said that pissed Nate off.

Nate ignored his brothers' taunts, turned away and continued to watch Althea.

He and his brothers had spent the morning moving livestock from two different pastures, and in that time his mind had been on Althea and the night they'd spent together.

A night that still burned hot in his mind. Images of her long brown legs wrapped around him as he stroked inside her body, her sweet mindless little mewls of satisfaction and the stamp of satisfaction on her face had all played hell with his attention the entire day.

He'd missed the looks his brothers had given him

and each other, his mind split between the job at hand and Althea.

Long after she'd drifted off to sleep, Nate had stayed awake, looking down at her, wanting all the pieces of the complex puzzle that made her.

The information she'd given, although succinct, had given him clues that had only added to her mystery.

Who was she, really?

As she slept, he'd gotten up once and gone into her bathroom. After using the facilities, he'd gone to the pedestal-style sink to wash his hands and spied a small black bag. Indecision filled him.

He hadn't wanted to go through her things, yet curiosity about her overrode the knowledge that prying through her things wasn't cool.

He decided to hell with being cool. He lifted the bag and peered inside.

Her wallet was there, and he stopped, feeling guilty. Prying wasn't his style, and neither did he appreciate it in others.

Besides, he'd rather she be the one to tell him who she was instead of learning this way. He wanted her to trust him enough to do that.

He'd returned to bed and found her in the same position, with his pillow hugged to her chest. He gently moved the pillow and repositioned himself so that it was his body she curled around instead.

When she placed her hand on his chest, Nate had lifted it, turned her hand over, again caressing the calluses on them. She was complex, he'd thought, a frown bisecting his brows.

A woman who obviously was no stranger to hard work. Yet one who painted her toenails bright pink.

And then there was her wallet. Although he hadn't opened it, the designer label of both it and the matching purse hadn't made sense to Nate. He had seen no other evidence during the weeks she'd spent at the ranch that she was the type of woman who would pay that much for a simple accessory. But it was obvious that she was used to the finer things in life.

Nate was picking up on the small inconsistencies, ones that alone didn't mean much but together were beginning to paint a picture of a woman whose past held more than a few secrets. Yet she had given it all up and chosen to move from place to place. Why?

More important, why did he care? She was just a momentary distraction. He ignored the instant inner mocking voice that called him a liar.

"Hey, boss, you want me to get the new hand settled in the barracks?"

Nate's attention was drawn from watching Althea's antics with the cows when his foreman approached. His brothers had given up on riling him and left moments before.

"He got all his paperwork in? Everything check out okay?" Nate asked absently, his mind still on Althea. Jake Stone had been the foreman for over ten years, and Nate as well as his brothers had learned to trust his judgment on anything to do with the ranch, including hiring.

Jake was only a year older than he was, had grown up around the ranch from the time his father was the foreman, taking over the job when his father retired. He knew the Wyoming Wilde and its operation as well as Nate and his brothers.

"Hmm, yeah, just about," he answered, and paused. Nate glanced up and saw his sandy brows knotted.

"What's up?" he asked.

"It's just something about this one that seems a bit odd to me."

"Yeah? In what way?"

"On paper he checks out good and all. Top-notch references across the board. In fact almost too damn good. But when he came by today to sign the paperwork…I don't know. Just seemed odd, is all. Now, I know looks ain't everything, but he sure as hell didn't look as though he'd ever done a hard day's work in his life." The cowboy took off his hat and ran his hands through his dampened, short blond hair, spiking it over his head, before placing his hat back.

"I can't see him getting his hands dirty, with the way they looked, much less riding a bronco. 'Less it was one of those mechanical ones at the Laredo," he finished, referring to one of the more popular country-and-western bars in Landers.

"Hold on…he rode *bronco?*"

The foreman shrugged his broad shoulders. "Hell, that's what it said on his résumé. According to his résumé, he's done everything from milking cows and branding to a stint riding bulls."

"Where is he now?"

"Went into town to get his stuff. With how soft his hands looked, he probably went to get a manicure while he's there," the man mumbled, and Nate resisted the urge to laugh.

"When he gets back, let me know. I'll have a look at him, check him out."

"Will do, boss."

Satisfied with that, he turned to leave, but before he could, Nate stopped him.

"Looks like Althea enjoyed herself today."

When he saw the knowing look on Jake's face, he wished he'd kept the comment to himself.

Jake barked a laugh. "Yeah, she did! She worked just as hard as the men. You got a keeper with that one, boss," he said with a broad wink.

"I'm not sure how long she'll be here. I just wanted to make sure she didn't get into any trouble while we were away."

When his foreman gave him the same *yeah right* look as his brothers had, Nate squashed the need to explain or knock the grin off his face, the same shit-eating grin his brothers had given him over the course of the day. He'd learned from trying that with his brothers that the only thing it was guaranteed to do was make it worse.

Chapter 15

Althea brought her gloved hand to her forehead and absently wiped away at the sweat, running a glance over the newly turned earth.

It was early Sunday morning, and although she'd been given the morning off, Althea hadn't been able to stay in bed and do nothing. Torn, her emotions, her thoughts were all out of whack.

Making love with Nate had done that to her.

Coupled with the fact that although she'd seen him from a distance over the last two days, the two of them hadn't exchanged a word. To say he was avoiding her was putting it mildly. To say she was confused and more than a little irritated was a given.

After eating a small breakfast she'd gone outside. Wandering around the cottage's small, enclosed backyard, she'd found a shed not far away. Curious, she'd ventured inside and to her delight the shed was fully stocked with planting supplies inside a variety of air-tight containers.

Inside she found seeds and bulbs, all carefully labeled. One of the many activities she and her father had enjoyed together was gardening, and from as early as she could remember, no matter where they'd been living they'd had some type of garden. Even in the apartment they'd lived in when she was barely school age, she fondly recalled the small herbal garden they'd kept on the balcony of the two-story apartment.

It was an unusually warm day, and perfect for planting. Althea selected a few of the seeds and bulbs, ones that were right for planting in early spring, added them, along with some supplies, to a small wheelbarrow and made her way back to the front of the cottage.

The cottage itself was testimony to very careful planning, the meticulous design of the cottage itself as well as the furnishings. That final touch was missing, curb appeal, she'd thought with a grin, and set to work.

Now as she sat back, she carefully lifted the flower bulbs from the container and placed each one in the holes she'd dug before moving on to the next. Humming, Althea put on her earphones and turned up the sound, contemplating the changes in her world over the last few weeks.

Sunday morning was the day Nate and his brothers gave the men time off. Some used the time to sleep in after a night spent out in Landers—his brothers included—while others chose to visit family and attend church services.

The one day Nathan had to sleep in, not waking at dawn as he normally had to, sleep remained elusive. All because of Althea.

She'd started helping Lilly with the afternoon meal, and those times Nate had carefully made sure he was nowhere around, although he'd been the one to suggest to Lilly that Althea help her.

He felt like some adolescent boy whenever she was around. Gut all twisted in knots, heart thumping when he caught a glimpse of her…and completely unlike what he was used to, what he was comfortable with.

He had it bad. The woman was getting to him.

But he needed time. Time to come to terms with his growing attraction.

After a solitary breakfast with no one around, even Lilly taking the day off, and his brothers no doubt recuperating from a night out in Landers if they were home at all, Nathan gave up trying to fool himself that he could allow it to continue. Thoughts of Althea were playing in his head round the clock.

And avoidance had never been his style.

He went to the barn to saddle his favorite horse for a ride. Maybe that would help him clear his thoughts, get his mind right. It always had in the past, even after Angela left. Even then, he had easily managed to submerge himself in his environment, his world, where nothing and no one had been able to penetrate his thoughts.

But the trip to the stable only reminded him of Althea as well, as he passed the stall of the Arabian he'd bought from the old rancher.

Whatever magic Althea had performed on the animal,

if he could figure out how to bottle it to sell he'd make millions.

Not only did the horse now allow him near, it also allowed Nate to saddle and ride it, to his surprise.

His intention was to go to the south pasture, check on the new calf, but halfway there, he turned around and headed to her cottage. Reining the horse in he slowed his pace, and stopped short within a few yards of the cottage.

He frowned, looking across the short distance to see her knee-deep in dirt, her small body bouncing, earphones on as she worked. It was then he noticed what she was wearing on her head: his hat.

He remembered the day he'd given it to Angela. It was the same day she'd left both him and his hat in the cottage, along with a note saying she couldn't go through with their engagement, that ranch life wasn't for her.

Expecting the accompanying anger, he found instead that the memory garnered no more than a fleeting thought, simply something that happened in his past.

Althea, garden shovel in hand, was digging deeply into the earth, head bobbing as she listened to her music, totally immersed in her work.

Just like a kid, playing in the dirt.

An unknowing smile lifted one corner of his mouth as he observed her.

Althea sat back and observed her work, a satisfied smile on her face, thinking how beautiful the flowers would be when they bloomed. She closed her eyes, inhaling deeply, imaging the beautiful fragrance they'd give in late spring. She couldn't wait to open the window and let the scent wash into the cottage.

Her shoulders hunched and she sighed.

She doubted she'd be around to see the fruits of her labor.

In fact, she didn't know if she'd even be around to see the first stems break free of the earth, much less get to see the flowers bloom.

She forced the dismal thoughts away. "No matter. Someone else will have the pleasure," she murmured, patting the earth before with a sigh, then turning and gathering her things.

As she was placing everything back inside her wheelbarrow, she paused, one hand grasping the small shovel tight, a prickling sense of awareness telling her that she was no longer alone.

She didn't need to turn around to know who was there. Licking her lower lip, she closed her eyes, then casually glanced over her shoulder.

Her breath caught at the back of her throat; she slowly raised her eyes, her gaze traveling over him.

Larger than life, he sat atop his horse, the brim of his Stetson set low as he stared across the distance at her.

Her body ran hot and cold, a wave of goose bumps rushed over her skin. She slowly exhaled the pent-up breath through her nostrils.

It felt like a lifetime instead of two days since she'd last seen him.

She rose to her feet and removed the work gloves, turning to fully face him. A tight fist clenched in her stomach.

* * *

Patting the horse on the rump after tying it to a large beam near the cottage, Nate's eyes never left Althea's. Even from his distance away, he could feel the tension radiating off her in scalding waves. He knew she was more than aware that he'd purposely kept his distance from her. Justifying it in his mind, the need to sort out his growing feelings for her, was no excuse. He knew it. But he'd needed that time.

Lot of damn good that had done.

As he stood finally less than a foot away from her, all of his careful thinking, rationalizing, flew out the window the minute he was near her again.

A smile tilted the corner of his mouth. He reached down and fingered the speck of dirt on the end of her nose away.

Without a word, he brought her close. Enveloping her in his arms, he burrowed his nose in the curve of her neck, inhaling her unique scent deeply into his lungs.

Her arms came out hesitantly before wrapping around his waist. His eyes closed briefly, his hold on her tightening. "I'm sorry," he said low, the words barely above a hoarse tone.

He felt her slight trembling and brought her away from his body, far enough so that he could see her face.

He caressed the soft line of her cheek with the back of his hand, answering when he saw the look of question in her liquid brown eyes, "For avoiding you."

She raised a brow. "Oh, is that what you were doing? I didn't even notice," she quipped, one dimple flashing in her cheek.

"Didn't notice, huh?" he said, holding back an unexpected laugh. Bringing her close again before she could protest, he slanted his mouth over hers, pressing their bodies into tight alignment, tunneling one hand beneath her hair, knocking the hat off of her head as the other hand traveled down to cup her round bottom.

She moaned into his mouth, her arms lifting to curl around his neck, giving in to his kiss.

When he felt his erection grow stiff, aggressively pressing against her softness, he broke the kiss, reluctantly.

He wanted…needed…to lift her, take her into the cottage and make love, feel her sweetness wrapped around him until they exploded into ecstasy.

He also wanted to share something else besides his body with her. Something he hadn't wanted to do with anyone in a long time.

He looked away and motioned toward the ground where she'd been planting. "Are you done here?"

She frowned, nodding, pulling her bottom lip inside her mouth. "I hope it was okay. I didn't think to ask. I just—"

Nate shook his head. "No, it's cool." He held out his hand. "I'd like to take you somewhere, Althea."

She glanced down at his outstretched hand, a puzzled frown on her face as she looked up at him.

"Where?"

"I'll tell you about it when we get there. Trust me?" he asked.

She waited for a fraction of a second before placing her hand in his. Looking into his face, she nodded slowly.

"Yes."

The knot of tension broke with her acceptance of his hand.

Riding behind Nate with her arms wrapped around him, her legs and body close to his, along with the sweet morning air and the horse's unhurried cadence was a heady experience for Althea. It felt as though there were only the two of them, alone in the world.

She laid her head lightly on his back, wrapped her arms tighter around his lean waist.

During the twenty-minute horseback ride, the conversation had been as unhurried as the ride, interspersed with him sharing with her the history of the ranch, and his growing up, all of which Althea soaked up, eager to learn as much about Nate as she could.

The ranch was more than something he was part owner of, more than his livelihood, it was an intricate part of his makeup, who he was. All woven together into a fabric in the intricate tapestry of Nate Wilde.

Before her father had died, Althea had always been outgoing. After her father's death and her subsequent flight, she'd become used to being on her own. She'd adapted to her lonely existence and had become adept at batting away the loneliness.

Until she'd come to Wyoming Wilde. Now, everything had changed. All because of Nate, the men, the ranch… she found herself eagerly looking forward to what each new day would bring, found herself wanting…longing to be a part of a family again.

The thought was sobering.

"Here we are." Nate's voice brought her out of her musings. "This is where it all began."

She leaned around his big body, to see where he was pointing.

"Ohh," she breathed. "It's gorgeous."

Ahead was a stretch of land that was beautiful and breathtaking in its simplicity.

A long, wooden fence both separated and surrounded a small lake; a variety of trees and bushes were plentiful in the area, the lushness of the grass belying the time of season.

He quickly dismounted, reached a hand up to help her down.

"My brothers and I usually take care of the area ourselves, unless we're too busy."

After dismounting, Nate guided her up a long, narrow, pebbled path.

They walked past a penned area where several palominos were contentedly grazing, their tails flicking back and forth lazily as they ate.

When they drew nearer, they raised their heads, tossing them high, acknowledging Nate and Althea's presence before they returned to eating.

Althea turned her head, taking in the area. The Black Hills Mountains provided a majestic backdrop, the trees and small lake, the horses…it all gave a unique feeling to this part of the ranch, setting it apart from the rest of the land. Special.

That was how it made her feel, and she knew the place held a special significance for Nate.

"That's my father's house."

He pointed to a small log-framed house tucked

between a pair of seven-foot trees that were already blooming with large, white elegant flowers.

Althea drew in a deep appreciative breath. The contrast between the rugged area and the delicate, beautiful cherry blossoms on the trees was breathtaking.

"It's the first home he built when he bought the land."

When she felt his hand touch hers, she automatically placed her palm within his.

Together they walked along the pebble path toward the cabin, their bodies brushing against each other with each step. The closer they got, the more solemn Nate became.

She had become so in tune with him that she could *feel* the slight shift in his mood. It wasn't his silence that alerted her to a change. It was much more subtle than that.

Nate stopped, turned to face her, a contemplative look on his handsome face.

"This was also the first place my brothers and I called home. The first home any of us ever had."

Althea's eyes searched his, seeing something in his eyes…something indefinable, not happy or sad, but a curious blending of both.

He squeezed her hand once and released it before fumbling in his jacket to fish out a key and unlocking the door. When he opened the door, motioning for her to precede him, she walked inside.

After allowing Althea to go in front of him Nate followed, closing the door behind him.

He stayed just within the doorway, keeping his

attention focused on her as she walked farther inside the simple home he grew up in.

He leaned against the wall, folding his arms over his chest, waiting to see her reaction.

He and his brothers had preserved the cabin as it had been when their father was alive. Each piece of furniture, although old, mostly scarred and nicked, the scratches and dents on the walls, the old wood-burning stove in the center of the living area, were all reminders of their shared past.

Simply walking inside the old cabin brought memories of Nate's early life as a young boy to flood his mind.

Good as well as the painful ones. All were treasured.

He'd never brought anyone to the cabin, even the woman he was going to give his name, a woman he thought he'd live the rest of his life with.

The reasons he brought Althea to his early childhood home, the fact that he wanted to share a piece of his past with her, were ones he chose not to delve too deeply into.

Although she appeared to be a woman of no means, a woman without a home, there was more to Althea than who she presented to the world. Her manner of speaking held a soft sophistication that hinted she had come from not only an educated background, but he'd bet his ranch one where she'd been used to the finer things in life.

He saw her run her hand over the old fireplace before she lifted the lone framed photo set there and pushed away from the wall.

Once he stood directly behind her, he watched her fingers trace the old picture set behind the glass.

In the picture his father was in the background

watching as he and his brothers were bent over the fire, preparing to brand their first horse. He wasn't sure who'd captured the picture, it was so long ago.

Yet the memory of that day was branded in his mind just as though it were yesterday.

"That was a day I've always remembered, I'm sure all of us will," he said, laughing lightly as he stood behind her. "It was the first time Dad trusted us enough to go near his prize horses."

When she laughed softly along with him, he wrapped his arms around her waist. She instantly molded to him, relaxing within his embrace.

"And then there was the time we decided we were ready to break in one of Pop's new mustangs. Without a saddle. At midnight."

"At midnight?"

"Yeah," he said, running a hand through his hair, a sheepish look on his handsome face. "That wasn't one of our brighter ideas."

One story led to another, and by the time he'd finished, Althea was holding her sides in laughter.

"Oh God, enough!" she said, still chuckling at the antics of him and his brothers. "It sounds like you and your brothers loved every minute of it. It seems a pretty idyllic place for three boys to grow up," she said once her laughter had subsided, turning within his arms.

"We did," he said. "Times were hard in the beginning,"

"I imagine so."

"None of us knew what to expect, my brothers or Clint," he said, referring to his foster father. "Like I said, none of us really knew what family was all about."

He laughed lightly.

"But I wouldn't change anything about our life growing up here. It took a long time for me, for all of us, to feel that way," he said, the smile slight but still there, the love for his foster father there in his eyes, shining. "But even from the beginning this place has felt like home for me."

The memories he shared with her brought an easy, almost carefree expression to his normally somber face, transforming his features.

Althea had already thought he was finest man she'd ever seen, but when he smiled. Dear God. When the man smiled...

She inhaled a shaky breath.

Althea laughed at the stories he'd told her of growing up in the cabin with his father and brothers, as well as the fights they'd had.

"Me and my brothers, we didn't know what it was like."

"Like?" she asked, smiling up at him.

"To be in a family. Shilah was the only one of us who'd lived with his parents for long enough to even remember them. Holt and I, well, we'd never had family. Not real family, anyway."

He shrugged, lifting a shoulder in casual disregard, yet Althea ached for the boy he'd been, and longed to know what had happened to his own family. But she remained silent, knowing that he'd tell her in his own time. If he wanted.

He shook his head in fond memory and dropped his arm from around her waist, grabbing her hand, tugged her along the way, showing her the rest of the cabin and telling stories, some of which Althea just knew had to be exaggerated. By the time he was finished she didn't know the last time she'd laughed so hard.

With each story, she felt their bond, a bond she was helpless against, grow stronger. With each story, she yearned to know more about him, to know him in ways no one ever had. To know what happened to him as a young boy, why he had never had a family before Clint Wilde adopted him.

A jealous ping settled around her heart, making her pause, catch herself. She wanted to be the one, as his family had been, that he turned to in times of need.

They were in the larger of the two bedrooms. This one had a single bed and two bunk beds, the place he and his brothers called theirs. She turned to see him in the doorway, looking at her with a half smile on his wide, sensual mouth. She slowly walked toward him, trying her best to rein in the onslaught of emotion that was crowding in on her.

As she approached him, he pushed away from the wall and met her halfway in the center of the bedroom.

Standing inches away from him, her gaze traveled over his face. Cupping his face within the palms of her hands, she ran her fingers over the slight stubble that peppered his cheeks, his chin. She leaned into him as he pulled her against his body, his arms looping around her waist.

The memories he'd shared of his life as a young boy growing into manhood, everything he'd learned about ranch life and being a man, things he learned from Clint Wilde along with his brothers, had molded him into the man he was today.

The one gazing down at her, emotion blazing in his golden-brown eyes.

She tugged him close, brought his face down to hers and closed her eyes. She drew in a deep breath as she ran the side of her cheek along the roughened stubble of his.

This was the type of man she'd longed for her whole life. He was the man she wanted for her own.

The thought brought another painful stab to her chest even as her arms tightened around him.

Althea longed…ached, to be one of the people he loved, someone he was willing to fight for. To be a part of his family, to be his woman in every way…to have his children.

She drew in a sudden breath, squeezing her eyes tight.

He pulled away and brought his hands to the side of her face and closed his mouth over hers.

Although brief, the touch of his mouth against hers, the feather-light caresses, along with the emotions crowding in on her, made her body tremble. All too soon the kiss was over and he released her.

"Thank you," she whispered against his chest once the kissed ended.

He pulled away from her, a puzzled frown on his face.

She just shook her head, smiling, fighting the tears. "For sharing your life with me."

She smiled and pushed away, afraid that if she said any more she'd become a blathering idiot and scare the man to death.

"You gonna show me around the rest of the place?"

He didn't ask any questions, just nodded and led her out of the bedroom.

Taking her hand in his, he tugged her along with him.

"Follow me," he said, walking her toward the back of the cabin. Opening a door that led to a large open area, he brought her outside with him. Together, hand in hand, they walked for several yards until he stopped them when they reached a wrought-iron, intricately designed cross. Above the small tombstone was a small plaque pronouncing it to be the final resting place of Clint Wilde.

"Our father is buried here. He owned the property before the city's ordinance that dictated no burials on private property. Not that we would have cared, anyway." He laughed lightly.

Althea held on to his hand, tightening her grip, reaching out with the other to feather it over his thick forearm, the soothing gesture as automatic as it was unconscious.

"For the last six months we've been approached to sell the ranch," he went on quietly.

Althea's gaze flew to his. The thought that he would sell the ranch, something that was as much a part of him as his breath, brought an instant denial to her lips. He caught her look, shaking his head and leaned down, giving her a brief kiss.

"No, we're not selling. None of us would even consider the idea," he said, once the kiss ended.

"Oh…good," she said, not sure what else to say. It really wasn't any of her business if he or his brothers did sell, but the thought that they might was one that was upsetting to her.

"But our refusal to sell hasn't gotten through to Rolling Hills—the corporation that wants to buy us out," he explained. Then he continued, "They still haven't given up." With a sigh, he brought her close, placing her in front of his body. "Not only is this our living, it's our life. The only one any of us have ever known."

Althea leaned her head back against his broad chest, placing her hands on top of his where they were wrapped around her waist, content to be in his arms, hear his deep voice, the feel of it vibrating from his wide chest to her back.

"There's no other place on earth I'd rather be. No other place I could imagine I'd want to call home."

Althea sighed, taking in the view of the open land that stretched out as far as her eyes could see. The Teton Mountains in the background provided the perfect foil to the beauty of the landscape.

The Wyoming Wilde ranch was rustic, wild and untamed. Yet utterly beautiful.

Captivating. Just like the man whose arms were wrapped around her.

"No, I couldn't imagine you anywhere else but here, Nate," she softly agreed.

Chapter 16

Althea eased her body from beneath Nate's. Heat stole over her head to toe from simply looking at him, remembering the things he'd done to her, the way he'd made her body, mind and soul feel as he made love to her yesterday.

Everything about him was perfect, she thought, crazy tears burning the back of her eyes.

The sheet he'd used to cover their bodies had fallen down after she'd eased away, revealing his broad, muscled chest. His stomach was lightly furred, and the sprinkling of hair over his groin lay partially hidden beneath the sheet.

Despite his being asleep, the outline of his shaft, thick, pressed against the sheet, and Althea stopped herself from reaching out, fingering it, outlining its thickness in her hand, testing the weight of the round spheres that nestled behind it.

She drew in a shuddered breath and eased the rest of the way off the bed.

She picked up her discarded clothes, bundled them in front of her body, and after easing her T-shirt over her head she slipped her legs into her sweats.

As quietly as she could, she made her way to the door, the thick plush carpeting disguising the sound of her retreat.

Glancing down the long hallway, she quickly left his bedroom and practically ran the distance down the stairs to one of the spare bedrooms he'd shown her yesterday. Once inside the room she closed the door and leaned against it. Putting her hand over her heart, she felt it slamming against her chest as though she had just run a marathon.

"God, I'm a mess," she murmured, laughing at herself before walking toward the adjoining bathroom. Opening the shower stall, she turned on the water, allowing it to heat, before turning away to remove her clothes.

The previous day had been magical, from the time he brought her to his childhood home to the moment he brought her back to the ranch.

After returning to the ranch he'd brought her to the main house.

For some reason, being there with him made her weirdly nervous, all alone.

"Where...where is everyone?" Althea asked, once they'd walked into the warm, airy kitchen. Expecting to see Lilly, she'd found the room empty, no delicious smells of cooking greeting them as they came inside.

"She's probably at church still. She's usually there most of the morning. I think she mentioned today was her monthly usher board meeting," he said, watching her, a small smile playing around his mouth.

"Oh" was all she could bring herself to say, looking at everything but him. They'd been together, alone for the day, yet being in his home seemed so intimate.

"Your home is beautiful," she murmured, walking around the spacious living area near the kitchen.

"Thank you."

The silence stretched out, and nervously Althea cleared her throat. "Umm…what about your brothers? I thought you all lived here…" she said, her voice trailing off when she felt his hands on her shoulders.

She closed her eyes and allowed him to turn her around.

He placed a finger beneath her chin.

"Am I making you nervous, Althea?"

She opened her mouth to deny it; saw the humor in his eyes and felt an answering grin tug at her own lips.

She shrugged, smiling sheepishly. "Maybe. A little."

He brought her close, his expression become serious. "Look, I'm not going to pretend I know what's going on with us, beyond now. This is new territory for me as well."

Althea frowned. "But I thought…" she stopped, realizing that he'd never told her about his fiancée, something she'd learned from Lilly. "I mean, Lilly told me that you were once engaged, but that's all she said."

His frown increased. "Yes, I was. But I've never felt like this about anyone. Even Angela."

At that her heart leaped, thumping hard against her

chest. When he brought her closer she eagerly went into his arms, not asking for any more than he was willing to give at the moment.

It was enough.

When he'd asked her to stay the night with him, she'd agreed. The two of them had then gone up the stairs, arms twined around each other, and spent the rest of the day and night in bed together.

Althea released a long breath and finished undressing, staring at her reflection in the mirror. Running a hand down her body, over her breasts, she remembered the feel of Nate's big hands caressing her last night, the feel of the slightly callused skin as he ran them over each of her breasts.

She released one of her breasts, her hand trailing down her stomach before stopping at the juncture of her thighs. Brushing a hesitant hand over the soft curls, she swallowed against the sensation, the memories of what Nate had done to her the previous night playing over and over in her mind.

"Is that your normal MO, Althea…running?"

Seconds before he spoke, Althea had felt a prickling heat warm her skin, the same one she got every time he was near. With a start, her eyes flew open.

A glance at the door and her eyes widened before she stumbled, a hand reaching out to steady herself against the marble countertop.

Nate stood in the doorway, clad in only his boxers, arms crossed over his wide chest, a deep frown marring his perfect face.

"I…I didn't, wasn't running," she said, embarrassment

at being caught touching herself making her so her nervous her mouth felt like cotton.

He nodded a head toward the shower. "You'd better get in the shower before it gets cold. My brothers will be up soon. Sometimes it takes a while for the water to reheat."

His eyes ran over her, again making her skin heat.

Instead of leaving the room as any decent man would, he kicked the door closed behind him and advanced into the room.

Althea took several steps back until her back bumped against the glass shower door.

"What are you doing?" she asked, although the question was silly even to her own ears.

It was obvious what he was doing.

Keeping his eyes on hers, one side of his wide, sensual mouth turned up, he pulled down his boxers, kicking them away from his legs as he walked closer.

She inhaled a quick breath when his cock emerged, thick, hard, thumping against the hard ridge of his tightly muscled abdomen.

Without a word he opened the shower door and turned to her. He held out his hand and waited.

She stared down at his hand and up at him.

It seemed to be a recurring theme of theirs, she thought, finding unexpected humor in the situation.

Althea couldn't read the look in his unfathomable eyes, but the intensity…the intensity of his stare reached out and grabbed her. Made her want to take his hand and let him lead them wherever he wanted, whenever he wanted… She shut her eyes, briefly and swallowed.

Did she even have a choice? she thought before taking his hand.

He drew her into the shower and closed the door, the moist, sultry warmth immediately surrounding them. She watched with heavy-lidded eyes as he reached for the bath sponge, squeezed a healthy portion of the scented liquid soap into it, brought the sponge up to her neck and smoothed it on her overheated skin.

She closed her eyes and moaned.

"Does that feel good, Althea?" he asked, his voice a rumble, pouring over her just as the warm cascade of water sluiced over her warm skin.

She moved her head to the side, allowing him to run the soft sponge down her throat, and answered, her voice a thready whisper, "Yes."

"Good," he said, turning her so that her back was flush against his chest. "I only want to make you feel good. Do you believe me, Althea?"

She wanted to believe him, everything he was saying, everything he was implying.

Wanted to believe that this incredible man wanted her, needed her...would protect her. And love her.

She wanted it so badly she battled against the emotion pounding into her as he was stroking inside her.

She felt the strength of her need for him in every fiber of her body, in every part of her mind, body...soul.

She couldn't fight the tears that burned the back of her eyes as he stroked her, her body going up in flames.

Tears due to the realization that no matter how much she cared for him, and as much as she wanted to tell him everything, to unload her burden onto his wide shoulders and give him everything that had been weighing down on her for so long, to trust in someone other than herself…in the end she couldn't endanger him or his family to Reggie.

He meant too much for her to do that.

She was in love with him.

The depths of her feelings caught her unaware, hitting her hard. She bit down on her bottom lip to stop the words from tumbling past her mouth until she felt the metallic, coppery taste of blood inside her mouth.

Althea leaned her body back against his chest.

He raised her and lifted her so that her bottom bumped against his groin.

She whimpered, the sound barely audible, when she felt his big hand trail around to her mound and brush back and forth over the curls that guarded her entry.

Held her breath when she felt him separate her. Bit the bottom of her lip as two of his fingers toyed with her clitoris, rubbing it slowly back and forth before a finger invaded deep inside her body.

"Nate…" she whispered and cried out when his finger plunged in and out of her while his thumb continued its sensual assault against her clitoris.

"Will you let me make you feel good, baby?" The question was asked in a guttural whisper against her neck.

"Yes…."

She cried out in denial when he withdrew his finger, only to arch her body sharply when he angled her and slowly entered her, feeding her his shaft in a hot, short thrust.

"Nate!" she cried when he withdrew and plunged deep, so deep inside she felt his sac tap against her bottom. Again he dragged himself out of her, only to plunge deeply back inside her clenching heat, her mewling cries mingling with the sound of the water raining down on her. She frantically clutched at his hands on her waist, her body still sensitive from last night's lovemaking.

He grasped her hands and placed them on the shower wall. "Keep your hands there," he instructed, licking the underside of her ear, tugging the lobe in his mouth and biting down.

Not hard enough to hurt, but enough that she felt the stinging caress to the core of her femininity.

Oh God, she wanted to believe him, Althea thought, panting as he began to slowly pump inside her body, his strokes slow, measured. Wanted to believe he cared a fraction for her, what she felt for him.

"Do you believe me, Althea?" he asked, even as his depth of stroke had her crying out, her head thrown back, accepting his wild loving. She couldn't say anything. She could only accept the here and now, what he was doing to her, the way he was making her feel. She knew she'd remember it for the rest of her life.

As he made love to her, tears of love and need mingled with the shower water streaming down her face.

When Althea didn't respond, Nate bit back a growl of frustration. His hands tightened on the soft skin of her waist as he stroked inside her, pouring all of his frustration, his need for her to give in to him, to believe that whatever demons hunted her were his demons to battle as well.

He didn't know what to say, what to do, to break

down the wall she refused to let down. A wall he was determined to get beyond.

The only thing he knew was that she was his. And if she would only allow him this, he was going to give her everything he had. Eventually he'd break her down, make her admit she cared for him, let him in.

Bending down he covered her completely, his chest sliding against the wet smoothness of her back, his mouth hovering against the nape of her neck. He closed his eyes, running his nose against her skin, inhaling her unique, intoxicating scent as he stroked deep inside her.

"Let me in, damn it," he growled, deep in his throat, his need feral.

The demand came out of nowhere. But the feel of her clenching down on him, the way she welcomed him inside her femininity was turning him upside down, making him crazy.

"Nathan…" she whimpered even as she ground her sweet bottom against his invasion. Even the sound of her voice was making his mind and body go supernova.

"Baby, you are in…what do you…" She stopped, her breath coming out in gasps as his strokes increased. "What do you want?" she screamed out the last words when he angled her on his shaft. "I'm…I'm afraid." The admission was torn from her, calming him enough that he eased his strokes, his hands losing the tight grip they had on her waist.

"Don't be. Never that, Althea, please, baby…"

One hand left her waist and cupped a breast, thumbing the tightening nipple, while the other trailed around her waist, down her thigh to caress her, before moving back up, seeking her sweet, hot nub.

He found what he was looking for. He stroked the tiny bud hidden deep in time to his thrusts.

Her whimpering cries grew louder, bouncing off the shower walls, echoing throughout the bathroom. When he positioned both hands back on her waist and lifted her higher on his shaft, he drove down in one well-orchestrated move and she broke.

"Yes, yes…oh God, Nate, yes, yes, yesss…." Her cries ended on a harsh wail when he brought her face around enough so that he covered her mouth with his, pummeling into her sweet core in short, staccato thrusts.

Deftly he flipped her around to face him fully, losing connection briefly before tunneling back inside her warmth. She stared up at him, her mouth partially opened, the ends of her nostrils flaring and water spiking her long lashes as water streamed over her.

Cupping her bottom, he brought her flush against him, readjusted their bodies and slanted his mouth over hers, pulling her luscious full lips into his before allowing them to plop out.

He licked and sucked her mouth, his tongue darting between the seam of her lips, just as his shaft sliced between the seam of her creamy opening.

"Nate," she whispered, her eyes feathering closed.

Her breaths came out in panting breaths of air against his mouth, their tongues performing a sensual battle of their own as their undulating bodies ground and writhed against each other in the ultimate dual.

Groaning low in his throat, Nate pulled her as tight as

he could against his body, massaging the rounded firm globes of her bottom, squeezing and molding them as she rode him.

"Yes, yes…oooh," she moaned, her breathy little cries making him grit his teeth to hold back the orgasm that hovered.

Digging into her at a new angle, one that allowed him to go deep, he couldn't get close enough. He felt nearly crazed with his need for her.

Placing his hand between their joined bodies, again he found the core of her and as he stroked inside her, he rubbed her stiffened bud until she broke.

She screamed into his mouth, her body bucking against his as her walls clamped tight on his shaft so hard he felt his own release burning.

Releasing her clitoris, he tightened his hold on her small waist and pummeled into her, once, twice… rocking into her a final time before he too gave in, sending them both over the edge into bliss.

Their blended cries of release, one high, one deep, low, blended and merged into one mind blowing note of passion.

"I love you, Nate…God, I love you…"

Once her cries had died down to sighs, Nate reluctantly pulled out of her sweet, warm, heat. He felt his own heart mimic the chaotic beat of hers as their bodies remained close.

Blowing out a long, steadying breath, he rested his forehead against hers, allowing his body to calm and his heartrate to return to a semblance of normalcy.

Kissing her forehead, moist from the shower and her own sweat, he opened the shower door.

Stepping out of the shower he grabbed one of the oversize, plush white towels and wrapped it haphazardly around her before he lifted her high in his arms and carried her back to his bed.

Placing her in the center, he took a moment to look at her, her skin rosy from the shower and their lovemaking, her lids closed, her full, sexy lips partially opened.

A frown pulled his brows together, echoes of her cries finally penetrating his brain.

Had she cried out her love for him? Or had it been something he'd conjured up, something he'd wanted to pull from her, wanted for her to say to him…

Her eyes, low, slumberous and satiated, lifted and she stared back at him.

Again he felt his cock stir, thicken.

It wasn't enough.

He dropped the towel he'd quickly wrapped around his waist and joined her on the bed.

He covered her with his body, kissing the side of her neck, running his nose down the side, inhaling her unique smell into his senses. "Althea." Her name came out in a coarse whisper as he licked the sensitive spot beneath her earlobe before pulling away and looking down at her.

She raised her hands, brought her palms on either side of his face and softly ran them down his cheeks. He turned his face into her hands and kissed them before removing them, placing them high above her and securing them with one hand, the other going down to part her thighs.

He saw her eyes widen when he centered himself between her legs, his cock pressing against her moist heat.

He didn't know if he would ever have his fill of her, if he would ever have enough of her…

"Nate…" she cried in a low, soft, utterly feminine voice.

Her back bowed high off the bed when he began to slowly enter her. He took his time, filling every inch of her with him…filling her up in a way that no other man could touch what was his.

Filling her until he didn't know where he started and she began.

Their lovemaking was slow and easy. He kept her body flush against his as he rocked inside of her, his pace lazy, sensual, his thrust measured and steady.

He took his time with her, refamiliarizing himself with every inch of her body. His hands skimmed lightly over her dewy soft skin, her full, perfect breasts and over her hips, before grasping them in his hands, pulling her willing body even closer to his as he leisurely made love until before long the feel of her tightness clenching down on him, skin to skin, no barriers between them, became too much.

Even as he lengthened his stride, his strokes became more demanding, demanding that she give him all of her, until there was no more to give.

Until she had nothing left for any other man.

Until she admitted she was his.

Chapter 17

"I love you, Nate..."

The words filtered into Althea's sleeping brain, forcing her eyes to open.

As soon as they did she squinted against the early-morning light peeking through the wide-slatted blinds in Nate's bedroom.

She sat straight up.

In Nate's bedroom.

She glanced down at herself. Her naked self...

She quickly shut her eyes and with a groan flopped back down on the bed, the events of the night before coming to her mind.

She kept her eyes tightly closed as though that would erase the things she and Nate had done together throughout the long night before.

As though that would make the images go away.

Althea drew the sheet away from her body and

touched the slightly reddened skin on her thighs, wincing at the ache from her touch.

She blew out a breath and sat up, leaning against the headboard.

God, could it be, had she told him she loved him? Had she admitted to him what she felt?

If there was any doubt in her mind about her feelings for Nate, last night he'd stormed through every one of her objections, his lovemaking so intense she had to tighten her legs against the memory of the feel of him inside her body.

Nate, like his brothers, didn't love lightly. But when they did…if they did, it was real.

Althea pulled her legs up until her knees touched her breasts and wrapped her arms around them before resting her head on top of her knees.

But did he love her?

The sound of raised male voices pulled her away from her mental musings. She sat forward in the bed and crawled down until she was at the foot, straining to listen.

She was only able to pick up bits and pieces of the conversation. She heard Nate's voice, quickly followed by Shilah and Holt, the three men in what sounded like a heated discussion.

She rose from the bed, and walked toward the door, curious as to what they were saying.

"How many are sick? Dr. Crandall on his way?" Nate asked, running a hand through his hair, eyeing each of his brothers. "Can't you two handle this?" he asked. It was too early in the morning for this crap. Besides, his thoughts were solely on Althea, wanting nothing more than to crawl back into bed with her, wake her up, and make love to her all over again.

Their lovemaking had been intense, raw and earthy. Beyond the lovemaking, she made him feel things he never thought he'd feel for a woman.

She was everything he wanted in a woman. Although she'd only been on the ranch for a little while he knew what he felt for her was real. That his feelings for Angela had only been a pale imitation of what he felt for Althea.

His only concern now was if she loved him as much as she loved the ranch, as much as he loved her.

The realization of his feelings hit Nate swiftly, bringing him up short.

He loved her.

Loved everything about her. From the stubborn look that would cross her face, to the impish light that entered her eyes when she was teasing him…to when her features softened and the stamp of satisfaction played upon her face after they made love long into the night.

Damn.

His love for her had been there, growing with every day he spent with her, every moment in her company, for longer than Nate admitted to himself. It had snuck up on him and sucker punched him right in the gut. And he hadn't even seen it coming.

"Yeah, well I think you need to see this."

His brother dragged him out of his musings, and he forced himself to listen as Shilah filled him in on the situation.

They'd been notified that after a random testing of

meat from the local packing plant. The test had revealed that the meat was tainted, suggesting that the animals it had come from were sick.

Although the meat hadn't been identified as coming from Wyoming Wilde, the men had immediately had Dr. Crandall come out and perform a full testing on all the cattle, particularly their recent purchase of prize cows, to make sure they were all clean.

Dr. Crandall had assured them the animals were healthy, but had sent several blood samples out overnight express, pulling several strings to get the results quickly, to rule out sicknesses that would only show in full blood work.

Nate felt his gut clench as he listened to his brothers, forcing all thoughts of Althea and his love for her, from his mind, temporarily. "The results?"

Shilah shook his head. "Clean. Didn't come from us," he said, and Nate released a relieved breath.

"And why wasn't I told about this?"

Holt shrugged a shoulder. "Didn't want to get you worked up, at least unless there was something to worry about." He looked at Shilah, including him in his comment. "We thought you've had a lot of other things on your mind, lately. No need to get you involved unless needed."

Nate ignored the reference to what…or who…had taken up most of his thoughts over the last few weeks. He was under no delusions that his brothers didn't know what was going on between he and Althea.

He was no longer trying to hide it from them. They'd know soon enough when they realized he was moving her in with him.

"So, what's the problem?"

"Wouldn't be a problem if we didn't have Rolling Hills on our ass," Holt replied, both his expression and tone of voice grim. "Those sons of bitches are just waiting for an opportunity…"

"An opportunity they'll be waiting for until hell freezes over," Nate cut in, his voice equally grim.

The Rolling Hills Food Corporation had moved into the area, setting up their main plant in Landers, less than six months ago. In that time, they'd bought many of the surrounding ranches from family-owned operations, and had on several occasions approached Nate and his brothers about selling.

Their latest offer, although lucrative, the men wouldn't consider, their love for the Wilde Ranch more than any monetary compensation could compare with. Sending the corporation a firm no, they'd thought that had been the end of it.

But it hadn't. Soon after their latest refusal, the men had begun to come across roadblocks they'd never encountered before, red tape that hadn't been there before when selling their stock. Small instances, yet when added up they had begun to take a small toll on the ranch's finances. They were still doing well, expanding and buying more livestock, the ranch prospering and doing better than it ever had, yet the men were concerned.

And now this. The issue of bad meat was nothing anyone took lightly, and the men had always been extremely careful in making sure their animals were healthy.

Before the recent issues with Rolling Hills, none of

this would have been a cause for alarm, particularly as Dr. Crandall had given them a clean bill of health. However, with the corporation after their ranch, they didn't put anything past the megacorporation and knew that any rumor started about bad beef, and even a hint that it came from them, could be a death sentence for Wyoming Wilde.

"The cattle is cleared, but I think we need to check into this before any rumors start," Shilah said, mirroring Nate's thoughts.

Nate agreed, realizing that as much as he wanted to spend the day in bed with Althea, making love to her, he also needed to accompany his brothers to protect their ranch.

"Look, baby, something's come up. I have to go. I want to stay with you—"

"Go," Althea cut in, rising from the bed to meet Nate as he entered the bedroom. "Don't worry. I'll be here when you get back."

She met him halfway into the room, leaning into his embrace as he hugged her, running his head back and forth over the top of her hair.

She felt the tension in his body when his arms tightened around her, and heard the thread of anger mixed with anxiety in his deep voice.

She leaned away from his embrace and glanced into his face, seeing his features tight with worry. She brought a hand up, easing the frown away from his wide forehead, smoothing her fingers over his knitted brows.

He captured her hand, brought it to his mouth and kissed her fingers, closing his eyes briefly.

"Promise?" he asked, his voice husky.

She forced a smile onto her face, batting away the nagging thought in her mind, the thought that Reggie was somehow involved in what was going on with the animals, that he'd found her. That she was the cause of the trouble the men were facing.

He brought a finger beneath her chin to bring her face up to meet his eyes.

"You're incredible, you know that?" he asked, his eyes roaming over her face. He shook his head. "You coming into my life has been the best thing to happen in a long time—I don't know how or why it happened, I'm just glad it did," he said, cupping the back of her head and pulling her close, kissing her with swift yet sensual precision before letting her go.

Althea felt the sting of tears burn the back of her eyes. She smiled shakily and tried to look away from him.

He forced her to turn back to him, the frown on his face returning, deepening.

"What's this for?" he asked, thumbing away a tear she hadn't known streaked down her cheek.

She smiled, shaking her head. "Nothing. Just overly emotional I guess. Must be that time…you know," she finished weakly.

He stared down at her a fraction longer. Opening his mouth to speak, before he could say anything they both heard his brothers' voices outside the door.

He brought her close and kissed her again. When he released her, he placed his hands on her shoulders, forcing her away enough that he could really look at her.

"I've got to go," he said, his tone reluctant. Althea nodded her head, swallowing down the emotion that threatened to overwhelm her.

"While I'm gone, go to the cottage and get your things together," he murmured, against the side of her forehead, kissing her.

Her eyes flew to his. The look of dismay and what she *thought* he meant must have shown in her eyes.

"God no, not that," he said, laughing lightly and brushing a kiss over her opened mouth. "I want you here, with me. I want your face to be the last one I see at night, and the first one I see in the morning," he murmured, his eyes dark with an emotion she had to close her own against.

With a soft cry she pulled his head down to hers. The kiss was quick, but so hot she stumbled when he finally released her. He thumbed beneath her chin, forcing her to look at him. "Okay?"

Unable to speak, she simply nodded her head in agreement.

"But when I get back…when I get back, you and I are going to have to talk. Really talk, Althea. It's time," he said, his words and tone of voice sending a fresh wave of anxiety to pool in her gut.

She knew her reckoning day was coming. He wasn't going to allow her to evade him anymore. He would demand the truth from her. All of it. It was there in his eyes. He'd wring from her everything she had. He wouldn't settle for less.

"Yes," she agreed, her voice a whisper. With a final

kiss, she watched him as he turned and strode out of the door.

Watching him leave, an uneasy feeling settled in her stomach.

Chapter 18

Althea spent the morning helping Lilly as she busily worked her kitchen with the precision of a military drill sergeant, calling out orders to both Althea and Joseph, the young ranch hand she'd roped into helping them, as they prepared the afternoon meal for the men.

Although she listened with one ear, glad for the work to help keep her thoughts away from Nate, if only temporarily, her mind was a million miles away, filled with thoughts of him, the two of them, and her current situation. What to do…

From Lilly she'd learned more of what the men were facing, what was going on with the ranch. Nathan had already told her a lot about Rolling Hills Corporation and their ongoing fight to try and buy Wyoming Wilde, and the lengths the men believed they'd go to achieve that.

And although it seemed that somehow Rolling Hills

were the ones behind it all, as the men suspected, a part of Althea dreaded that Reggie was caught up in it somehow…that he'd found her and was out to sabotage her newfound happiness.

She mentally shook her head. No. It couldn't be, she thought, remembering the few times she'd thought she'd seen Reggie on the ranch, only to discover it wasn't him.

She was so used to looking over her shoulder, so used to never relaxing her guard, that her mind was playing tricks on her, making her see things that weren't there, giving him more power than he had.

She opened one of the commercial-size ovens before withdrawing the industrial-size pan of cornbread muffins she'd helped Lilly to make.

He couldn't be here, he couldn't have found me, she thought, her mind circling around the puzzle. Please, not yet.

She wasn't ready to leave yet. This was all too new, life on the ranch was hard yet satisfying in ways Althea had never felt…discovering a passion she never thought she'd have, with a man who was one of the most amazing men she'd ever known. A man she loved.

Please, not yet, Althea thought, sending the quiet prayer upward.

She just needed a little more time, time where she could capture each moment in her mind, like her own personal camcorder, to replay when she was again alone and on the road.

"Did you hear me, Althea?"

She turned away from the muffins, where she'd been

buttering the same one over and over for the last five minutes.

"I'm sorry, Ms. Lilly, I, I…" She stopped, shook her head. "Mind repeating what you said? My mind was somewhere else," she finished lamely, feeling off-kilter and uncomfortable as Lilly studied her intently from across the kitchen as though she was an object under a microscope, forcing a smile onto her face.

She stared at Althea a fraction longer before, with a sigh, she took off her oven mitts and turned to the young man helping them, instructing him to start loading up the food to take over to the canteen.

After she finished with him, she turned back and faced Althea, placing her hands on her ample hips.

"Come here, girl. We need to talk. Food's all done. Joe can take it to the men," she said, referring to the young ranch hand. "Want some?" she asked, referring to the tea she was in the process of pouring into a mug. Althea nodded her head, and after she poured her mug, the two of them sat down at the table.

She waited for Lilly to speak, not knowing what the older woman would say, but for the first time since she was a child, she wanted…needed to unburden herself to another woman, one older and wiser, like a mother.

As she sat there stirring the honey into her mug she patiently waited for whatever sage words would come from Lilly, ready and willing to listen, feeling as though whatever she would say would be exactly what she needed to hear.

"What in hell is wrong with you? Nate Wilde loves you. Really loves you. And here you are about to let it all go to hell in a handbasket!"

Startled, Althea's eyes flew to hers, nearly spitting the tea out of her mouth. "Wipe your mouth," she said, handing Althea a napkin.

"Excuse me?" She finally sputtered the words after wiping her mouth. Before she knew it a laugh tumbled past her lips, her laughter growing until she felt tears prickle her eyes.

The corners of Lilly's generous mouth twitched upward, and before long a husky laugh escaped. Within moments the two women were laughing together, the humor of the situation taking over.

Once their laughter had subsided, Althea leaned back, the grin still on her face. "I needed that."

Lilly reached across the table, took Althea's hand in hers, tilting her head to the side, again examining her, a small smile still in place.

Althea relaxed her guard. This time she didn't feel uncomfortable, she simply allowed the older woman to see the truth of what she was feeling.

The anxiety of Reggie haunting me, my growing yet confusing feelings for Nate…all of it.

She ran a thumb over the back of Althea's hand.

"Baby, it's all going to be all right. I know you've got some things you're holding close. I bet you've been holding a lot of things close, for a long time. Felt you had to," she said, and Althea looked away from her discerning eyes and glanced down into the dark amber tea.

"But it's time now."

"Time?" she asked, still not looking into her face as she stirred the contents of the tea, unnecessarily.

"Time to let some of it go. Time to believe that

someone loves you enough to help you. Time to stop running."

Althea swallowed back the tears, glancing out of the large, kitchen window that overlooked the expanse of the southern pastures of the ranch.

She waited for her to continue, waited for her to say more, but that was all she said.

It was enough.

"It…it's been a long time." Althea stopped speaking. Drew in a deep breath. "A long time since I've been able to put my guard down. A long time since I've felt at ease enough to do that, I guess," she finished, shrugging a shoulder.

Lilly continued to drink her tea, not looking Althea in the eyes, as though she knew how difficult it was for her.

"The man I became engaged to killed my father." The minute she uttered the words, actually spoke them out loud, she felt as though a life-size, heavy boulder of a burden had lifted from her shoulders.

Instantly, Lilly's hand tightened on hers. Again, she didn't say anything, simply waited for Althea to continue.

Althea worried her bottom lip with her teeth, debating how much to tell her, how much to share.

It had been a long time since she'd trusted anyone enough to do that. Before Nate, she hadn't thought she'd ever trust anyone ever, again.

In the short time she'd been with him, loving him, he'd made her begin to believe that she could do that.

Love.

She bowed her head, fighting back the tears.

She loved him so much, loved him as she never had loved another person in her life. She laughed softly, the sound painfully humorless.

Before she could speak, before she could make up her mind whether or not to open up to Lilly, unburden herself fully with the woman, Joe returned, coming into the kitchen ready to reload for the second trip.

It was enough to break the spell.

Enough to bring Althea back to reality.

She couldn't do it. She couldn't endanger Lilly… couldn't risk that Reggie would find out and hurt the woman.

Lilly looked at her, not blinking, not moving, waiting.

After a short time, she nodded her head, squeezed Althea's hand one final time. Althea saw the effect of her words, caught the sheen of tears in her eyes, but when she rose, she looked down at her one final time.

"When you're ready, baby. When you're ready…"

Althea nodded, unable to say more.

Chapter 19

As he and his brothers suspected, someone, more than likely Rolling Hills, was trying to set them up.

Dr. Crandall had met them at the south pasture and gone over the test results with the men carefully before they'd gone together to inspect the animals.

After that they'd checked on the animals' feeding area, as well as all the equipment used, carefully checking and rechecking, pulling out their own testing equipment and making sure their livestock and equipment was clear.

It had taken the entire day, but by the end of the evening, all were assured that they were clear. Saying their goodbyes to Dr. Crandall, relieved that the ranch was clear, relief set in.

When his brothers had asked him to come out with them, share a beer at one of their favorite watering holes in the local town, Nate had declined, eager to get back to Althea. Although he'd had his full concentration on dealing with their situation, she had been on his mind nonstop throughout the entire day.

The drive back would have gone quickly, as he'd driven in his pickup and not gone by horse, had it not been for the weather. Although the day had started out fairly clear, as early evening set in, storm clouds had set in along with it, and now, as he headed home, the rain was coming down in torrents, obscuring his vision so badly he'd had to lower his speed to a near crawl.

By the time he made it back, the rain was battering against his truck, and with relief he cut the engine and raced into the house, eager to see Althea.

Coming through the house by way of the kitchen, lest Lilly chew him a new one for tracking her floors with rain and mud, he walked into the warmth of the kitchen. The house was quiet, the overhead light over the oven the only light in the large, open room. Not wanting to wake anyone, Lilly's bedroom on the main floor, he figured Althea had to be upstairs in his bedroom waiting for him.

The thought of her, in his bed, waiting for him to come home, sent a rush of need through him, and the desire to see her, bury himself inside her warm, honeyed depths and make love to her until the early-morning sun peeked through the blinds, hurried his steps even more.

He wanted to forget, for a moment, the threat to the ranch. Wanted to think of nothing but Althea, the two of them together, lost in their own world.

Quickly shaking off the rain clinging to his jacket, he shed it, tossed it on a chair and raced through the house, taking the winding stairs that led to the bedrooms three at a time before he reached his bedroom.

Before he could open the door, his hands were already on the buttons of his shirt.

"Baby, I'm home," he called out, striding into the bedroom and stopping.

The room was empty, the bed freshly made, with no indication she had lain in it.

"Damn it," he muttered taking off his Stetson and shaking it dry, briskly striding into his adjoining bathroom on the off chance that she was inside, taking a bath. His cock stirred at the thought, a grin beginning to tilt the corners of his lips, upward. If she was…

His brow furrowed when she wasn't there, a surge of anger going though him at the thought that she'd returned to her cottage.

"Althea's gone."

He spun around, spying Lilly in the doorway, her face devoid of expression.

"Gone? When? Where? Back to her cottage?" he asked, slowly walking into the room, not liking the look of worry and fear etched into Lilly's dark brown face.

She shook her head, holding out her hand. In her palm was a folded piece of paper.

He took the note from Lilly, scanned it, and biting out an expletive grabbed his Stetson from where he'd tossed it on the bed and slammed it on his head.

"When did she go?" he asked, the ends of his nostrils flared in anger, his mouth becoming a thin line as he clipped out the question.

"A couple of hours ago. But, Nate, the weather…it's getting worse—"

Nate wasted no time debating, wasted no more time with words. Weather be damned…he had to get his woman back, now. The need to have her safely where she belonged, in his arms, outweighed anything else.

Lilly stopped him before he could leave, her arm going to his thick forearm, the muscles bunched. "You might be able to catch her. Joe called the ranch a bit ago. Said she came into the shop because one of her tires had blown," she said, referring to the service station the young ranch hand coowned with his brother.

"When did he call?" When he saw the nervous way she wrung her hands, something completely unlike Lilly, he forced himself to soften his voice.

"How long ago, Lilly?" he asked.

"Joe said she looked really upset; scared. When he asked her if she was okay, she tried to pretend like everything was okay, but he could tell it wasn't. He saw her things in the backseat, her clothes and a box. Figured she was leaving the ranch. He asked her if she was and she didn't say anything, but he saw her eyes were red, and knew she'd been crying. He called here, looking for you. I told him to try and keep her there as long as possible until I could reach you." When she finished Nate cursed.

He was never without his cell within range, in case of an emergency. It was when he'd wanted to call Althea, let her know he was on his way home, that he realized the battery had died.

"That's when I went to the cottage. Everything is gone, Nate. And this note was left on the table for you," she said, motioning to the note he held.

"I have to get to her before she leaves and I never find

her." He knew the raw emotion beating down on him came through in his voice but didn't care. The thought of not ever seeing Althea again, the thought of her coming to some kind of harm, had created a chasm so dark, so bleak, he felt his gut hollow out.

"The weather is still bad, and it may have taken a while for them to try and locate a tire for her, at that time of night. With any luck she might still be there, Nate." Her voice was as grim as the situation.

After helping Lilly with the evening meal and helping to restore order to the kitchen, Althea had been at loose ends and decided to go to her cottage and pick up a few things.

The thought of what he'd said before leaving her this morning was like the lyrics of a song she couldn't get out of her mind.

Thinking about it made her believe, if only for a short time, that she could have a life with him, learning more about him…loving him.

Pick up the rest of your things from the cottage.

That's all he'd had to say and the idea had brought to mind images of the two of them doing the happily-ever-after thing. With two point two kids and a station wagon. Instead of the station wagon, knowing Nate it would be a couple of horses and a four-by-four…

She laughed at herself. He hadn't mentioned wanting it to be permanent, hadn't even told her he loved her. But for here, now…it was good enough for her.

She shrugged a shoulder, pretending a nonchalance to herself that was ridiculous even in her own mind.

Going to the cottage, she'd slowly began to remove

her things, fingering her precious few items she'd brought along with her, items that reminded her of her father and her life before everything changed horribly.

As she'd begun to remove her items, she opened the drawer where she'd kept the little black dress, the one she'd worn at the last formal event she'd gone to with her father. Maybe one day she'd be able to wear it somewhere with Nate.

The thought brought a small smile to her face, which quickly eased away when the dress wasn't there. Her heart began to pound harshly against her chest when after pulling out drawer after drawer, although she knew it wasn't there, she came up empty; the dress was missing.

Oh God oh God oh God…the litany went over and over in her mind, her heart now beating out of control. She went back to the drawer where she'd kept the dress and there, caught in the back, on the edge of the drawer, was a folded piece of paper.

With shaky fingers she eased it out and opened it. She scanned the neat, almost formal handwriting that flowed across the top. Two sentences. Two sentences and her stomach hollowed, nausea welling up from her gut and almost strangling her.

One day soon, you'll wear this again. Just for me, baby—

Fingers of icy-cold dread had threaded through her spine until the note slipped from her nerveless fingers and floated to the floor. Covering her mouth she ran, barely making it, to the bathroom.

Amidst tears of fear, rage and frustration all mingling into a crazy kaleidoscope of fear, her stomach bottomed out, her back bowing and arching as she emptied it into the toilet.

Taking in deep, gasping breaths of air, thinking her nausea was over, again she began to retch until there was nothing left inside. Weak, trembling, she could only lay her head down on top of the closed porcelain lid.

Within moments, adrenaline kicked in, forcing her off the floor. No time for self-pity, no time for debilitating fear…with speed born of desperation she ran through the small cottage, gathering and packing everything she could find, frantically double-checking her meager possessions to make sure she'd gathered them all.

Nathan…

She came to a sudden halt, right there in the middle of the living room.

How could she leave him… Closing her eyes, she dropped her bag and stumbled before falling down on the sofa.

"I want your face to be the last one I see at night, and the first one I see in the morning…"

She shook away the words, the meaning, the thought of what they could be if only…

No, God no, she wouldn't, couldn't think of him right now. She had to get away, had to go. Now. She'd come back when…*if* she could.

She swiftly stood, grabbed her things and left the cottage.

The rain, which had started moments ago, was now coming down in earnest, and squinting, covering her head with her jacket, she ran to the side of the cottage where she'd parked her car and quickly loaded it, before jumping behind the wheel. The car sputtered and coughed a few times until the engine kicked over.

Tears coming down in earnest, she drove as fast as she could away from Wyoming Wilde.

Chapter 20

Althea beat her hands against the steering wheel, cursing a blue streak that would make a drunken soldier on R-and-R blush when she saw the red arrow on her gas indicator point to red: empty.

Since her arrival at the ranch she'd driven her car twice. Both times had been for a quick trip to town to get personal items, and she'd had nearly a full tank when she parked it in the small garage.

How could it be on empty, she thought, again cursing. She *always* had a full tank of gas, as she never knew when she'd have to make a quick break and hit the road.

"Damn it!" she cried one final time before leaning back against the cracked old leather upholstery of her beat-up Toyota, wasted tears falling from her cheeks.

She squinted her eyes, leaning forward to scan the road, looking for a station. The rain was coming down so hard it was near impossible for her to drive at a rate much faster than thirty miles per hour.

She slowly crept along the deserted back road, breathing a sigh of relief when she saw a service station coming up on her right.

She pulled into the deserted, covered station, hoping it was open.

Jumping out of the car, she glanced around, hoping someone actually was working the station. She never used debit or credit cards for fear of Reggie tracing her. Cash was the way she'd bought anything she needed. If no one was there, she was up that creek without a paddle in sight. With relief she saw the open sign on the old building and quickly opened her gas cap.

It was then that she looked down on the driver's side at her tire and frowned. Placing the cap to the side, she ran her fingers over a long, jagged rip in the tire. Within a few miles it would be totally flat.

"God!" she cried, fighting back tears of frustration.

Again, she felt hopelessness begin to rear its ugly head, fear and loathing at the man she knew was responsible pelting down on her as much as the rain now fell in wild torrents from the sky.

A crack of thunder, coupled with a man's voice directly behind her, had Althea turning, crouching and assuming a fighting position that would make any world-wrestling athlete proud.

"Hey, hey, Miss Althea, it's just me!"

Relief swept over her when she looked up to see Joe, the young man who'd helped Lilly earlier in the kitchen, frowning down at her, his hands out and up, as though in surrender.

"I'm sorry, Joe. I'm just a little on edge," she said, quickly rising. Hearing the shakiness in her own voice, she cleared her throat.

"Is everything okay, Miss Althea?" he asked, his young face earnest.

She swiftly nodded her head. "Yes, I'm fine. Just need some gas. And this patched," she said, motioning toward her tire.

"I didn't know you worked here," she went on, trying to bring normalcy to her situation, her glance sliding away from his when she noticed how intently he was looking at her.

"Yeah, me and my brother bought the place a few months back. Worked like a mother fu—uh, worked real hard," he said, his face turning three distinct degrees of red as he corrected his language, temporarily placing a small, genuine smile on Althea's face for his efforts. "Saved for three years…but it was worth it," he finished, his face beaming with pride.

"So, what do ya need? Just gas? I can pump it for you. We're one of the last full-service stations—" As he spoke, she caught the way he was trying to peep into her backseat, where she had all of her possessions. She subtly readjusted her body to block his view.

"I also need to get this fixed," she broke in, tempering down her impatience as she motioned toward her tire. "Think you can help me out?"

"Shouldn't be too hard. Let me take a look." He walked around her to hunch down, check out the tire. Again, she caught him trying to peer inside her car after he'd risen.

Althea moved, situating her body again against his prying eyes. Finally he got the hint and moved away.

"Come on inside. I'll have this fixed for you in a jiffy. Should just be a patch job. There's some coffee in the lobby, help yourself, Miss Althea. I'll just need your keys."

With a grateful nod, she'd handed him the keys and walked inside the "lobby," which was giving the small, dingy area way too much credit.

"Beggars can't be choosy," she said, thankful to be out of the rain and cold.

After taking longer than she wanted, Joe came back to tell her his brother had to get the type she needed in town.

"The *type* I need?" she asked, confused. "Aren't they pretty much standard?" she'd questioned him.

"Uh, I'm afraid there's a…uh, nail in it. Patch won't do. Gotta replace the tire," he replied, his face reddening.

"How much will that cost?"

"Not much. I'll get you fixed up. Just gonna take a little longer. We ain't got the new shipment of tires yet. My brother's already in town, he can pick one up and bring it on in." He palmed the back of his neck and rubbed it, glancing away from her, both actions telling.

Something wasn't right. Yes, she knew paranoia was her new best friend, but still…

"Look, maybe I can just go a little farther with it on a patch. Make it to one of the stations in town—"

"No, Miss Althea. I got this. Let me take care of it for you. Please." He reached out to place a hand on her arm as she turned to go. "I promise it won't be long and you can be on your way. I don't want you driving any farther with that busted tire," he said, his voice almost pleading.

After he'd assured her they'd have her car fixed as soon as possible, she relented and went back inside the lobby.

After nearly an hour, he finally came back inside and handed her the keys. When she asked for the bill he shook his head. "Don't worry about it. It's on the house."

"I couldn't—"

"Please. Don't worry about it," he replied, his eyes searching hers. "Just promise me you'll head back to the ranch. It's getting really bad out there."

From his expression she knew that he'd contacted someone from the ranch, and she needed to do the complete and utter opposite.

Mentally crossing her fingers, she promised him she would.

"Where is she?"

Joe turned from beneath the hood of the car he was attending to, facing Nate as he burst into the station, his eyes wild. Dropping the dirty rag in his hand, he hurried to turn down the music blasting from inside the truck.

"I tried to keep her here as long as I could, boss, but—"

"How long ago did she go?" Nate cut in, past the young man's stammering.

"'Bout thirty minutes ago. Ain't no way she coulda got far in this rain—"

Before he could end his sentence, Nate was back inside his truck, peeling out of the station.

After leaving the house, he'd made record speed, adrenaline strumming, fighting like hell to ignore the fissure of raw fear that he wouldn't arrive in time to find her.

But still, he'd arrived too late and she was gone, out of his life.

No, he couldn't think that. He drew in a deep breath, even as his heart continued to race. As he drove the deserted road, his eyes constantly scanned the side in case she'd had to pull over.

She'd told him she didn't love him in the note she left. Told him that it was time to move on, she no longer wanted to stay and was growing restless. That ranch life wasn't for her and she needed something new.

His first instinct had been to put his fist into the nearest wall, had it not been for the memory of her dark, chocolate-brown eyes as he stroked into her, her soft cries…the way she called out her love for him.

His mouth tightened.

Hell, no. She loved him. If he had to drive to hell and back, he'd find her, force her to admit the words she'd cried out had been true. Force her to tell him what had caused her flight.

He came to a fork in the road and stopped, slamming his hands against the steering wheel in frustration. She could have gone either way. Depending on which way she went, the road would take her to two different directions on interstate eighty.

He needed his brothers. He lifted his cell, and with a curse remembered the battery was dead.

"No!" he bellowed, driving across the highway divide and stopping, debating which way to go, absently plugging his cell into the car's charger.

A flash of bright pink beneath the overpass caught his attention from his peripheral vision. He impatiently pressed the button to roll the window down, and less than a hundred yards away, he made out a small figure in front of a car, hood raised. It was her.

Relief made his hands tremble as he made a sharp U-turn. Flipping around to reach her, he was out of the truck seconds after slamming the gear into Park.

Althea had little time to do anything besides release a loud yelp before thick, muscled arms wrapped around her.

She went into autodrive.

Violently twisting in his arms, with a strength born of wild fear and desperation she managed to lift her arms from the tight hold, clamp her fingers down onto the arms that held her at the same time that she gave a backward head butt. She heard the satisfying thump as her head made connection with his and redoubled her efforts to get away.

"Sssh, stop fighting me, damn it! Baby, stop, it's me… God, baby it's me!"

It took a several moments more before realization dawned on who held her and her body went weak. Spinning around, she looked into Nate's furious face.

A cry fell from her lips before they were covered with his.

Gathering her into his arms, he held on tightly, his hold on her punishing as he ravished her mouth.

Desperately she clung to him, standing on tiptoe as she clutched at his shoulders, never wanting to let him go. Finally he released her, pulling away, his eyes gleaming with an emotion so intense it reached out and nearly suffocated her.

"I—I…" She stopped, not sure what to say.

He didn't give her the opportunity. He had her bundled and beneath his arms, guiding her to his truck before she could protest. "One of my brothers will come back in the morning and get it," he said when he saw her look back at her car.

"Where…where are you taking me?" Althea finally spoke, once they'd been driving for several miles.

"I know a place not far away. We can settle there for the night."

He didn't even turn to look at her when he answered, his profile stern, his full, sensual mouth set in a straight line. When he said nothing more, she sighed and turned back around to stare out into the jet-black night, the moon's glow the only illumination.

The rain had begun to ease, but a lot of damage had already been done to the area. Several lights had been blown and many of the lighting posts that peppered the two-lane back road had been uprooted from the ground.

After what seemed like hours but had probably only been twenty minutes or so, he turned into a gravel lane and cut the engine.

Althea looked out into the nearly pitch-black night, unable to see much beyond the window.

"Stay there, I'll come and get you." He jumped out of the truck, slammed the door and seconds later was opening the passenger side, placing his hand beneath her elbow to guide her out.

The rain and wind had died out to a quiet whisper, leaving that strange, eerie quiet that always came after a storm.

Althea suppressed a shiver and held on tightly to Nate, barely able to see a foot in front of her, but trusting that he knew where they were going.

She heard the creaking steps beneath them moan under their feet when they reached a small cabin. No sooner than he had her safely inside, Nate turned to her and stripped her out of her coat, quickly followed by the thin, damp T-shirt she wore underneath it, and went to work on her jeans.

They were also soon tossed on the floor beside them. She stood before him wearing nothing but bra and panties, the cool cabin air penetrating her wet skin, her body shivering, the drama of the day, the damp feeling of her skin finally catching up to her, making her body shake violently as she stood before him.

Although the cabin was dark, the moon's glow lit the naked windows, and Althea drew in a deep breath when she saw the angry, smoldering look in his light brown eyes.

"Nate…" She tried to turn away from him, tried wrapping her arms around her body to protect herself from the cold…and him.

He advanced on her, pinning her to the wall, bracing his arms on either side of her body, effectively caging her in.

When she tried to move her head to the side, again wanting to avoid his eyes, he removed his hand from the wall and grasped her firmly beneath the chin, forcing her to look at him.

Unable to prevent it, she flinched.

When his jaw tightened her eyes were drawn with a fatal fascination to the small tic in the corner of his sensual mouth.

"You ran from me. And now you're afraid of me as well, Thea?" His tone was frigid; so sharp it felt colder, sharper than the frigid wet weather she'd just come from, cutting deep into her flesh.

"No...I, I..." she stammered, and stopped. His angry stare, his very presence, took away her ability to move.

She swallowed, her heart now thudding like a master drum against her chest.

He pulled away enough so that he could see her. His hot stare glided over her body, the heat reaching out to smother her in its intensity.

"And then you leave me nothing but some bullshit note telling me it was just a fling...that what we had wasn't special and that it was time to move on? I meant so little to you that you couldn't even wait around to tell me in person?" Although his voice was low, each word stabbed at her heart like a well-slung dart.

He moved his hand, ran his fingers down the side of her face, and again she flinched, the action nowhere near the sweet, hot and loving caresses she'd grown to expect...ones she'd become addicted to.

She shoved at his chest and then covered her breasts with her hands, turning away from him, feeling exposed and emotionally raw beneath his molten glare.

Impatiently he batted her hand away and forced her to turn back to face him.

"You don't get to do that. You gave up the right to do that when you told me you loved me," he said, roughly, replacing her hands with his and covering her breasts. Thumbing away the cup of her bra he pulled one breast out and ran his fingers over it, caressing her lightly. Toying with her.

Her eyes widened. So she hadn't imagined she'd told him how she felt, the last time they made love. Oh God, he knew...

Althea bit back a moan, fought against the pull he created, the need for him to make love to her, not just now, but for the rest of her life.

He bent his dark head down and engulfed her breast in his mouth, biting down on the tight nub, hard enough that the sting raced through her body.

"Please, Nate..." The whispered plea fell on deaf ears.

His stinging caresses and laps of his tongue made her arch her body away from the wall, pushing her breast farther into his mouth.

His hand snaked down her body and pushed inside the silk band of her panties. He sought her out and she moaned when he caught her tight bud, her head rolling to the side at the dual, erotic caress.

He suckled her breasts, pinched and rolled her tightening clit until she grew frantic. Her body was no longer hers to control; she grasped his head, pulling him closer, both mind and body dizzy with frantic need.

He broke away, pushing her away from him, and she cried out in denial, her eyes snapping open.

Impatiently he snatched off his shirt and swiftly unsnapped his jeans, shoving them past his hard muscled thighs and down his legs, taking his shorts along with them.

His cock sprang free, thick, long and hard.

Althea stared at it, her stomach clenching in a knot. Slowly her eyes trailed up his body and met his gaze, then she turned away. His anger was there, tightly leashed but evident in the set of his features. The ends of his nostrils had a slight flare, his eyes carried an emotion that blazed fury, mingled with another emotion, one that frightened her more than the anger.

Love. It blazed there, despite his fury. A love so real, so strong, Althea felt like running, far and fast. A love she was afraid would consume her in its intensity.

In a flash he was on her.

His hands came out and grasped her shoulders, turning her around to face him. She stumbled, her knees buckled and she fell to the floor.

Before her body could make contact, he'd caught her by the waist, easing the rest of her downward fall.

"That's another thing you don't get to do. Run away from me. Ever again." The words were a hoarse whisper against her ear as he covered her back with his warm, naked chest.

His tongue snaked out and lapped a rough, hot kiss down her neck, over her spine, ending at the indenture of her waist. When she felt his fingers dig into the flesh at her hips and heard the sound of her panties ripping, she closed her eyes, her hands braced on the floor, her head hung low.

"Nate, baby…please…" The rest of her words were

cut off in a strangled groan when one thick finger snaked past her moist folds and embedded itself deep within her body.

When he withdrew his finger, she heard his grunt of satisfaction. "You want me. You always do, no matter what. I'll take that, for now," he growled. Before she could react to his words she felt the slow, hard invasion of his shaft as he rocked inside of her.

Her body took over from there. Rearing back against his invasion she ground against him, her body on fire with need and love for him. One last time…she'd make love with him one last time before saying goodbye.

The thought brought the burn of tears she'd felt hovering at the back of her eyes to the front, before one lone tear trickled down her face. She silently cried, even as what he was doing to her body brought shivers of delight to course down her spine.

One last time…

Forever…he could make love to this woman for the rest of his life.

As Nate held on to her waist, his fingers holding her body steady, he plunged and retreated into her willing, moist cave. As she moaned, grinding her body against his, bucking back against him, he knew that it would never be enough with her.

He wanted…needed her for the rest of his life. She was as necessary as the air he breathed. Without her, he couldn't survive.

He rocked into her, his thrusts growing stronger with each drive into her welcoming sheath. Crazed, wild with the feel of her walls closing and clamping down on his shaft, it was a long moment before her soft cries penetrated the hazy cloud of lust surrounding him.

He gritted his teeth, forcing himself to ease his thrusts.

He needed to see her beautiful eyes as he made love to her. Needed to see if there was love in them. That what she'd said was true.

She might be able to hide, dodge and pretend with others, but not with him. Not when he made love to her. When they made love every emotion showed on her face.

He deftly eased out of her. Grasping her hips, he flipped her so that she lay on her back. Centering himself between her legs, he bumped them farther apart and eased back inside.

Her groans, soft, sweet as he was fully embedded inside her, spurred him on, made him so hard for her he felt nearly out of control, making him go as deep as he could within her wet, warm, willing body. He didn't stop until he was so deep inside her body he felt the end of his shaft invade her womb.

He blew out a grunting breath of air and slowly flexed his hips, dragging out of her clenching heat until the tip of his cock hovered at her entry before driving back, deep.

As he began his sensual drag and pull into her body, he glanced down at her and saw that she'd shut her eyes and her face was turned to the side on the thick rug, her long lashes resting against her high cheekbones.

Her eyes were closed, he knew in an attempt to shut him out.

Not this time.

He took her hands within his, raised them so that they lay flat on the rug, and held her tight.

"Open your eyes, Thea." The demand was made and she responded immediately.

Slowly her passion-filled eyes opened and their gazes locked.

Her dark eyes were glittering with a dark sheen of tears. They held so much emotion it made his heart clench. Made his hold loosen on her hands. He drew out slowly, feeling her clenching heat on his shaft, and slowly pushed back inside her, forcing away the desire to plunge into her over and over until she was weak and stake his claim.

"Oh God, Thea…what are you doing to me?" The words were torn from him as they stared at each other, their gazes locked as they made love, neither one of them able to look away.

She shook her head and said nothing, her hips slowly moving, accepting him into her body.

The gesture was so vulnerable and helpless it made every male instinct to protect what was his rise and surge to the front. Her vulnerability was what did it to him. Broke him down on levels he never thought were possible. Made him realize just how much he loved her. How bleak his life had been without her, and how much more bleak it would be without her in it.

He adjusted her on his shaft and with painstaking slowness ground inside her. He wanted to feel her. Every part of her.

He wanted to savor every part of her, saturate and drown himself in her. He wanted to make her his for all time.

* * *

Althea felt the change come over him and opened her eyes slowly, meeting his intense gaze. When he first entered her body, she'd felt his energy, impatient…angry. Now as he stroked inside her, his tempo changed, the look in his eyes making everything in her go soft.

She licked her lips, wrapped her legs around his waist and brought him close.

"Oh God, Nate…I love you," she said, the words a soft whisper and totally unexpected. But she didn't regret them. She felt her eyes burn, felt the tears as they slipped down her face. "I love you so much."

He bent down, captured her lips with his as his strokes grew stronger. When he brought his mouth to her breasts, her body arched sharply off the floor and she moaned softly.

He grasped her hips, grunting as he stroked inside her. His strokes grew demanding, his thrusts painfully sweet as they became more powerful. Although the rug they lay on was soft, she knew she'd have bruises from the power of his thrust, but she didn't care. The only thing that mattered was what he was doing to her, the way he was making her feel, both inside and out.

"Oh God, Nate, Nate, Nate, Nate…" She shut her eyes, light-headed as the pleasure he gave her spiraled and grew out of control.

Frantically she clutched at him, her nails scoring his back. He reared his big body away from her, the muscles in his neck standing out sharply as his body tensed, his grip on her hips punishing.

On and on he pressed and retreated, rocking into her,

his thrusts hot, hard and satisfying until she screamed out her release.

"I love you, Althea!"

She heard his roar from a distance as she gave in to the mind-blowing release, her body no longer hers to control.

In that moment, before she closed her eyes and allowed the orgasm to sweep her away, she looked up at him, past the dew of sweat that ran in streams down her face, and knew her fate was sealed. It had been the moment she'd met him.

She belonged to him, mind, body and soul. For as long as he wanted her, she was his.

Chapter 21

Althea's eyes parted, opening slowly. The strength of the orgasm had nearly made her pass out, lost in his strokes, his kisses, his love. It was a long time before she could even open her eyes.

When she did, it was to find his light brown gaze on hers. At some point he must have gotten up and found a sheet, and now it lay over the both of them.

He lifted her hand from where it lay on his chest and brought it to his mouth, placing a kiss in the palm.

"When I came back home and found you gone, everything faded to black. I never want to feel like that again. Why did you leave, Althea?"

The question was straight and to the point. But she'd expect no less from him, that was who he was.

She sat up and turned to face him, worrying her top lip with her teeth. Running a hand through her hair, she didn't know where to begin, what to say, where to start.

He reached up and brought her back down to the rug, pillowing her head with his chest.

He ran a hand over her hair. "Just start at the beginning. I promise whatever you tell me, whatever happened, won't change the way I feel about you, baby."

Althea played with the soft, springy hairs peppering his hard chest, trying to figure out in her mind how to start.

Taking a fortifying breath, Althea began to speak, sharing things with him that she hadn't told anyone, things she hadn't told Lilly. Things she'd never said out loud to anyone, afraid to speak them, as though saying it aloud would give them more power.

She hadn't known how she'd feel even as she poured out her story to Nate. Expecting to feel fear, instead she felt free, freer than she had since her father had died. It wasn't until she finished that she realized the burden that had begun to lift after she spoke to Lilly had cracked open even further. When she stopped, he turned her around to face him.

There was a frown on his face, as he pulled he tugged her closer.

"And this man, this man your father mentored— Reggie—has been after you ever since?"

"Yes, no matter where I go, he ends up hunting me down. And…and he's found me again." She paused, took in a deep breath and plunged in.

"There…there were a few times I think I saw him at

the ranch. I put it down to the state of hyperawareness I've been in for the last couple of years."

Althea then told him of the times she'd thought she'd seen Reggie on the ranch, only to feel silly when it was just one of the ranch hands.

"I thought it was all in my mind. God, I've been running so damn long…looking over my shoulder for what seems like forever. I thought I'd finally lost it, was seeing things that weren't there." She stopped, pausing when his frown increased. "I know, I know…it was all in my—"

He stopped her, placing a kiss on her mouth. "No, baby, it might not have been. Describe him for me," he said, and Althea felt that queasy feeling return, her belly filling with an anxious knot as she described him to Nate.

"Son of a bitch," Nate mumbled. Jumping from the floor, he raced over to his jacket in the corner of the room and retrieved his cell phone.

Praying he'd gotten enough juice in the thing, he turned it on, thankful that two of the cells indicated it had recharged enough in the car to place a call.

"Baby, what?"

He turned to her. She had the sheet he'd covered them with wrapped around her body, her hair a disheveled mess over her head. Although the situation was critical, his instincts telling him that the man she was describing was the same guy his foreman had mentioned, he felt his cock stir again at the picture she presented.

The stark white of the sheet was startlingly erotic against the dark brown cream of her skin. With her hair tousled, her lips puffy from his kisses, she was the picture of any man's erotic dream come to blazing life.

He kept his eyes on hers as he phoned his brother, briefly asking him about the ranch hand he'd hired, the one with the odd résumé. As he listened to Holt tell him he'd check on him, the other part of him was fully concentrated on Althea.

He saw the moment her eyes widened, saw the swift breath she took, her tongue snake out to wipe across her full sensual mouth the longer he stared at her.

He spoke a few minutes more with his brother before he ended the call, and with his eyes still on hers, he opened the old chest and withdrew several pillows he'd spied earlier before coming to join her on the thick rug.

After he arranged the pillows to his satisfaction, he brought her back down to lie on his chest.

"Is everything okay? What did your brother say?" she asked.

With him speaking to his brothers, the reality of her situation had returned, ending the euphoria from their lovemaking.

"Seems like the new hand may have been this mother—guy, Reggie. I've got both of my brothers hunting him down now. He won't get far."

"You think he's still at the ranch?" Althea asked, one part of her fearful that he was, the other part hoping that he hadn't been on her trail since she'd left.

"Your brothers…Lilly," she said and he stopped her, kissing her softly.

"Don't worry about my brothers. They can take

care of themselves and Miss Lilly. They've alerted the foreman and they're heading toward town where he's staying to get his ass."

His voice had taken on a hard edge, one that sent a shiver to slide down her spine. She almost laughed, thinking that for once she feared what they would do to Reggie once they found him. Almost.

She snuggled closer to Nate, feeling protected within his strong arms.

He feathered his hand over her hair and she felt him place a kiss at the crown of her head.

"You won't have to worry about him anymore, baby. My brothers and the others will get him. He'll never hurt you again, I promise."

She held him tightly, content to lay within his arms.

"Do you love me enough to marry me, Althea?"

The question made her jump, her head bumping against his chin. She heard his grunt, and pushed away, her eyes wide.

"Marry…" She stopped, cleared her throat. "You want to marry me?"

"Well, not if you keep abusing me," he said, rubbing his chin, a sparkle of humor in his eyes. "But barring that, yes, I want to marry you. I've never loved anyone the way I love you. I never knew a love like this could exist. Never thought I could ever have someone like you in my life. The way you make me feel. The way you laugh, your stubbornness, your humor…everything about you, I love."

He stopped, brought her close. "Please. Marry me, Thea… Please don't make me walk this earth without you." The plea was raw, his voice barely above a rough growl. "I want to wake up to you each morning..."

"I want your face to be the last one I see at night," she cut in, wrapping her arms around his neck, bringing his mouth down to meet her.

The kiss was long, sweet and satisfying. He drew away from her, cupping her face with his palms, his gaze searching hers.

"So this means yes? You'll marry me?"

She allowed the tears to flow unchecked and nodded her head to his loud whoop. Laughing past the tears, the laughter gave way to sensation when he lifted her, brought her back down on his body and slowly filled her.

"Nate? Baby? Where are you?" Althea called out. When she heard no answer, she wrapped Nate's coat closer around her body, wishing she'd thought to throw on something more to cover herself, and ventured farther outside.

After their last lovemaking, he'd lifted her into his arms, and walked through the small cabin before they reached a partitioned area with a bed.

It hadn't mattered to Althea that the bed was barely big enough for the two of them; she'd wrapped her body around his. The fear of the last twenty-four hours and Nate's lovemaking had been her undoing, and within minutes she was asleep.

She didn't know how long she'd slept, enough that the early dawn light was now peeking through the cracked blinds.

The cabin was so small that it was soon obvious

that he wasn't inside, and so she'd quickly grabbed the nearest piece of clothing, which was Nate's jacket, stuffed her feet inside her sneakers and gone outside.

"Nate, baby where are you?" she called out again.

She walked around the side of the cabin when she didn't see his truck, realizing he must have parked it on the side instead of the front. It had been so dark last night that she hadn't been able to tell where they'd entered.

"Nate, whe—" Althea stopped.

She couldn't move a muscle.

His body on the hard ground, unmoving. From the angle his head was away from hers, she saw blood oozing down his temple.

With a cry she raced toward him.

She dropped to the ground, her heart pounding frantically, her fingers running over the gash in his forehead as she brought his head into her lap.

She leaned down, reassured when she felt his breath fan against her face.

He was alive.

"Baby, baby, please, wake up, oh my God, Nate…" Her voice trailed off when she heard soft laughter coming from behind her.

She wrenched her head to the side, her heart seeming to come to a complete and utter stop. Slowly she raised her eyes to meet Reggie's dark, flat gaze.

He grinned at her, the smile not reaching his eyes.

"You've led me on quite the chase, baby, haven't you?" he asked, raising a finger at her and shaking it. "It's taken me a while, but I knew in the end we'd wind up together. The places you had me going…quite the journey you and I have been through together. But now we're back together, and nothing—" he glanced down at Nate, whose head was still pillowed on her lap, a sneer crossing his thin lips "—and no one will ever come between us again."

Althea was so afraid she felt nausea welling. But she knew she had to keep it together. Reggie was a ticking time bomb. Any minute he'd go off and with it, she knew he'd kill Nate and then her.

As he continued his loathsome diatribe, all Althea could do was just look at him.

His appearance was shocking, his clothes were ragged, the pants he wore frayed around the hem and his black loafers worn. She forced herself to remain calm, keeping her eyes on Reggie as he circled her, his speech growing more and more incoherent.

The hair on his face was spotted, not fully grown in, reminding her of some kind of mangy dog. Her gaze traveled over him, over his filthy clothes, the runover shoes on his feet and back up to his face.

A part of her mind separated from the horror that was taking place as she slowly stroked Nate's head in her lap.

Lost in grief, her misery had been fathomless after her father's death. She'd often relied on Reggie for everything from simple things, like reminding her what day it was, to the greater issues, such as taking care of her father's business. He had been her rock during a time of unrelenting pain.

Looking at him standing there, wiping the blood from the man she loved from his hands, a wild, strange crazy-looking smile on his face as he told her how happy they'd be together, the life he had for her…her fear and loathing for him, what he'd done, what he'd taken from her, transformed instantly into something frightening in its intensity, becoming a living, breathing entity of its own.

As though coming out of a daze, Althea carefully placed Nate's head on the ground and rose. From deep within a primal yell emerged, lodged deep within her throat, and she ran toward Reggie. She saw the surprise cross his wretched face just as she grabbed him.

With her hands clawed, tears running down her face, she reached for his throat.

Surprising him, she tackled him to the ground, going down with him. They rolled, her anger and fear giving her a herculean strength.

When they stopped, she spied a long, thick log of wood nearby. Scrambling away from him she crawled toward it and rolled around in time to see him coming after her.

She rose, the thick wood clenched tightly in her hand and swung at him, bringing him to his knees as she simultaneously jumped to her feet.

When he hit the ground, she was on him again. Straddling his body, she brought her makeshift bat back and swung again, this time catching him a glancing blow against his temple

"You crazy bitch!" he screamed, grasping his head with both hands, trying to protect himself against her blows, writhing on the ground in pain. Althea raised the bat back again, all the rage inside her bubbling to the front.

"You took everything from me!" she yelled, hitting

him with the wood, this time against his back. "My father, my life...you took it all away!"

Her chest rose and fell, her body heaving as she pummeled him, raining blows on his body as he writhed on the ground in pain.

"Tortured me for two years, followed me, attacked me, made me so afraid there were times I just wanted to curl up and die!"

She swung again, barely missing the connection with his face.

"Now you want to take my life from me again? Wrong damn answer...never again! Never again will I run from you!"

There was no answer from Reggie, his body still, unconscious, but Althea didn't care.

Althea thought back to how she'd felt the day the authorities had informed her that her father had died while on his boat, out on the water, alone, with a note admitting what he'd done, had taken his own life.

"You were the thief. You were the one who stole my father's clients' money. And you killed my father." Her last words were spoken in a coarse whisper, tears falling down her face, unchecked.

She stared down at him, her breath coming out in harsh, painful gasps above his unconscious body. "Now you want to take the man I love from me, the life I'm trying to build?" She raised the wood high above her head.

"Never again will I run from you again, Reggie. Never." The last words she uttered were barely above a whisper.

Ready to end his hold on her forever as she brought

the log down for the final blow, a strong yet gentle hand grasped her wrists, pulling her to her feet.

She turned with a cry and looked up into Nathan's beloved face.

"Enough, Althea…baby, enough."

Althea turned and beat against the chest of the man who held her, tears streaming down her face.

"I know, baby…I know. It's okay. He's not worth it. He's not worth your life," Nate said, and she cried even harder, burying her face into his chest. Hard tears racked her body until she could cry no more, her limbs grew limp. Had he not held her up, she would have fallen to the ground.

Had he not stopped her, she would have killed Reggie.

And he would have had the final victory in the end. Although she would have gotten her vengeance, she would have ended up paying a price for it.

She finally opened her eyes, pulling away from him to see both Shilah and Holt there beside them.

In her rage, her determination to end the terror Reggie had inflicted on her, she hadn't noticed Nathan's brothers' arrival. After a brief word with Nathan, both men moved toward the fallen man on the ground.

As his brothers pull a dazed Reggie to his feet, Althea heard them calling the local sheriff as they dragged him past them.

She barely gave him a glance, her eyes on the man who held her in his arms.

"You don't have to run anymore, baby. Never again," Nate said, the love he had for her blazing in his eyes. "I'll protect you, love you, cherish you for the rest of your life. If you'll have me," he said, emotion thick in his deep voice.

Tears ran down her face unchecked as she once more glanced at the man being taken away, the man who'd taken her father from her and had terrorized her for the last two years. A man from her past.

She slowly wrapped her arms around Nate, the tears of pain now mingled with those of joy, knowing the man who held her was the man of the present. The one who was her future.

She nodded her head, and he pulled her close, kissed her, before slowly releasing her.

"I want your face to be the last one I see at night..." he said, after he released her.

"And the first one I see in the morning," she finished, her voice thick with emotion.

Together they turned, slowly walking toward his waiting brothers and their bright, love-filled future.

* * * * *

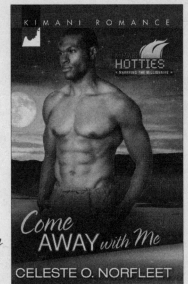

REQUEST YOUR FREE BOOKS!

2 FREE NOVELS
PLUS 2 FREE GIFTS!

KIMANI
ROMANCE ™

Love's ultimate destination!

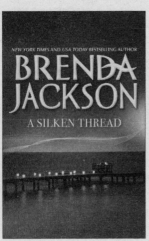